I0876028

Under the Grapevines

Under the Grapevines

Discovering Purpose Through Courage and Challenges

J. E. Daniels

Carpenter's Son Publishing
Franklin, Tennessee

Published by Carpenter's Son Publishing,
Franklin, Tennessee

www.ClovercroftPublishingGroup.com

www.JEDaniels.com

ISBN: 978-1968127497 print
ISBN: 978-1-968127-56-5 ebook

Edited by Ann Tatlock

Cover design by Suzanne Lawing

Interior Design by Virtual Graphics

Some events in this book are based on true occurrences and are altered and included here with permission. All names and circumstances have been changed to protect the innocent. Those who are guilty deserve no consideration. However, their identities have also been amended solely for the sake of the innocent.

Printed in the United States of America

Contents

Prologue

Flashing Lights Echo Danger

The darkness of the night crept through the kitchen like a slithering snake, as terror penetrated the room. Fear emanated from eight-year-old Penny's face. Her six-year-old brother, Ben, was scared and confused. He looked at the gun on the floor. Slowly, he moved his hand down to the gun, picked it up, and pointed it using both hands.

Penny was panic-stricken. There was a loud gunshot. Blood and pieces of flesh splattered Penny's face, hair, and body. She froze…

TWO MONTHS LATER

The ambulance lights flashed repeatedly across the exterior of St. John's Memorial Hospital at the emergency room entrance as the siren blared. The vehicle came to a stop. Two medics exited and removed Penny from the ambulance.

A hospital orderly yelled from the entranceway. "Have you got the burn victim?"

"No," Medic Hawkins shouted. "The medical transfer through social services."

Chapter One

Good and Evil Are Both Very Real

Dr. Judith Ramsey, an attractive, classy, but sincerely caring doctor in her late thirties, sat down on the edge of her desk and looked straight at Dr. Paul Brandon. He sat in an overstuffed chair across from her. Judith's light brown hair softly framed her feminine facial features and big brown eyes. Judith was elated, and it showed.

With a big grin, Judith began, "Do you realize, by my count, we've saved five marriages that were in absolute disaster mode in the last three months. Not just patching them up for a short time, not overlooking problems, nor allowing people to turn a blind eye to important issues. But we were able to teach the couples how to truly communicate and, more importantly, help them remember why they got married in the first place. That's five families intact. I've never had this much success so quickly."

Judith enthusiastically did a fist pump in the air. "I know we're not finished, but I think we make a great team. I am so thankful you left the Prison Rehabilitation Program, even though that was a terrific opportunity. This is how counseling should work. Paul, honestly, you come up with things I would never think of. And we helped all those children. We both know sometimes divorce is necessary in the long run, and, at times, even preferable. But if a family can truly be saved, that's a huge win and, especially, way better for the kids and teens that are involved."

"You're so right," Paul said. "These are the times it's rewarding to be a counselor. We deal with some rough stuff, and it's the successes that allow us to survive and keep our sanity. Truthfully, I've personally known eleven counselors who entered the field due to family issues they had to deal with during their childhood and the teen years. It makes me wonder what the overall percentage of counselors coming from bad childhood experiences truly is." Paul smiled. "You know what, this huge win deserves a celebration. I'll be right back."

Paul quickly grabbed a big package from his office and immediately returned to Judith. Paul was carrying a large, framed picture of Mickey Mouse. He gave a big smile and a slight chuckle.

"Why in the world do you have that enormous picture of Mickey?" Judith asked with a perplexed look. "I'm five feet seven inches, so this picture must be at least four feet tall."

Paul grinned. "It just arrived early this morning. Read these instructions on the printed plaque that goes with the picture, and you'll understand." He showed Judith a small frame he was also carrying.

While you are waiting,
please consider the following:
Walt Disney did ***not*** *have a great childhood.*
His ***not-so-great*** *childhood led him to create*
some incredible, terrific, inspiring, wonderful, and fun
adventures and entertainment for children that
we all love*.*
Walt felt childhood should be magical, fun, and
protected. It only happens once.
Of course, there is only one Walt Disney.
However, ideas, concepts, imagination, and
hard work are endless.

What wonderful creation or action can your ***not-so-great*** *childhood lead* ***you*** *to accomplish?*
It is well worth pondering.

"Why, Paul, you never cease to amaze me. That's

exceptional and brilliant!" Judith said with her mouth agape. "I never knew that about Walt Disney."

Paul breathed a sigh of relief. "So, you're okay if we hang this in the reception area? If not, it can go somewhere else, but I think it works best out there."

Judith quickly responded, "I would love it out there! It's profound and inspiring. I believe it will greatly benefit our clients. Everybody has had something hard to deal with in their life. This will help tremendously. It could help people focus on something positive instead of dwelling on and getting lost in the negative. And what's more positive than Mickey?" They both laughed.

"Walt Disney is one of my heroes," Paul admitted. "And his older brother, Roy, who made Walt's dream come true by completing Walt Disney World after Walt died early, at only sixty-five years old. Roy was considerably older than Walt and planned on retiring, but then Walt died. Some wanted to call it Disney World since Roy had worked so hard to make it happen. But Roy insisted it be Walt Disney World, because it was Walt's dream and conception. Roy made it happen, though. What a good brother he was. They had other brothers, but Walt and Roy were the only ones who were close that I know of."

Judith was fascinated. "I never knew any of that either. I love this idea. The challenge of making something wholesome out of a not-so-good childhood. Finding the strength to develop and create good out of a rotten past. What a phenomenal idea."

"I'm so glad you're okay with it. Thanks. I wasn't too sure how you'd feel," Paul admitted. "One of the maintenance guys, Jerry, will be by to put it up later. You get to pick the spot."

Judith's intercom rang, and she pushed the button. "Yes?" she asked.

The temporary receptionist, Becky, responded. "Please tell Dr. Brandon that his appointment's here, and" —Becky put her hand to her mouth and whispered— "she looks pretty bent out of shape."

"Thank you, Becky," Judith said.

Becky talked normally. "Also, please let Dr. Brandon know that I'm free this evening if he needs any filing or typing done or help of any kind. I'm available."

Judith quietly laughed and pointed at Paul. "I'll be sure to tell him." Judith turned off the intercom. "Let's face it, your incredibly handsome good looks, gorgeous hair, and charming smile must lead to numerous infatuations in our line of work." She paused. "Well, that would happen no matter your profession," Judith chuckled. "And you're a bit over six feet tall. That helps too."

Paul smiled at Judith. "You're very kind, but if you insist on using just anyone the temporary agency sends when Roberta's on vacation, the next time I'm leaving town, too," Paul stated emphatically with a grin.

Judith smiled, and Paul stood up to leave. He stared

Judith straight in the eyes. "Becky needs counseling as much as anyone who comes here."

Judith walked Paul to the door. "Oh, Paul, she's new to Springbrook and North Carolina. She's getting her footing, and it's only two weeks."

"That's easy for you to say. Seriously, when Roberta returns, please counsel Becky at no charge. I'll happily pay your fee," he declared, nodding his head.

Judith put her hand up to stop the door from opening. "So, why did you leave the Prison Program? You had such a great research situation there. That had to be hard to hand over."

"Ooooo! The bragging of the murderers was the worst. Many had no remorse whatsoever. But it will take longer to explain everything than we have; I don't want to keep Mrs. Benson waiting," Paul said.

Judith gave a huge grin. "Your concern is showing again."

Paul left Judith's office and entered the reception area. There were pictures of each of the ten counselors individually hanging on the large wall that read, "Welcome to Healing Hearts and Souls Therapy Practice. Our family of doctors is here to help you. We use a team approach to bring you the best possible care available." All of them were trained psychologists with various specialties, except for two psychiatrists—one elderly man and the other an older woman.

The team of doctors referred to everyone as a client rather than a patient. They felt it created a healthier atmosphere, especially since they used a team approach. Many people were familiar with the term "patient confidentiality," so when they decided to use a team process, it seemed like the best decision. However, all the doctors were to keep everything confidential and only discuss cases if they were currently involved with creating the best possible outcome.

Twenty-four-year-old Becky Perkins was sitting at the reception desk wearing incredibly thick and outlandish makeup, overdone hair, an extremely short skirt, and a tight, revealing blouse. As Paul entered, he saw Clare Benson wringing her hands and pacing like a caged tiger.

"Hello, Mrs. Benson, please come into my office," Paul said in his friendly manner, and then gestured the way. Clare Benson frantically walked into the office.

"I know I'm a little early. I'm so glad you're available," Clare said as she entered Paul's office.

Becky stopped Paul. "Dr. Brandon, can I get you coffee or something?"

"No, Miss Perkins. As I've said before, you need not wait on me. I am perfectly capable of getting my beverages. Thank you anyway."

Becky moved closer. "Oh, you have some lint on

your jacket." She tried to brush Paul's shoulder.

Paul motioned Becky out of the way. "Miss Perkins, please. That is not appropriate, and Mrs. Benson is waiting," he said and entered his office, closing the door.

Paul generally avoided using the first names of his clients or staff. This helped maintain a more professional atmosphere.

Becky watched Paul as the door closed. She hurried to the telephone and pushed three numbers. "Hi, Anna. Can you find out about Dr. Brandon? He doesn't wear a wedding ring, and there are no pictures of a family or females in his office. Oh, and find out about the cute UPS guy, too."

Judith, too, spent the next hour with a client, a routine and non-taxing visit. When Judith's client left, she walked out of her office carrying the picture of Mickey. "Becky, can you please help me find the best spot for this picture?" Judith said to get Becky involved.

"What? Oh, that's terrific! I've always loved Mickey Mouse," Becky admitted, and excitedly did little claps. It felt good to be included. "This is a fabulous idea," she added. "Mickey makes everybody happy."

"I agree." Judith smiled. "Let's play with some different spots. We need to check out which one works the best. Mickey is terrific."

Becky gleamed. She was glad to feel like a part of the office, even if she was only there temporarily.

Paul tried to hold back his anger and dismay. "Mrs. Benson, let me see if I understand what you are telling me. You are so distraught—as you put it, 'beside yourself'...."

"Yes, I am," Clare Benson emphatically replied.

"All because your fifteen-year-old daughter, Teresa, makes such 'a stink' about her stepfather opening the door every time she's dressing in her bedroom or she's in the bathroom?" Paul asked, absolutely appalled but trying not to show it.

"That's right," she responded.

"You said that the dinner party you and your husband attended last night was ruined?" Paul asked.

"Completely ruined," she replied.

Paul was progressively more appalled. "You said that driving to the party and home, the only discussion was of what an ungrateful brat your daughter is?"

Clare Benson heartily nodded.

Paul continued. "This has happened before, and your daughter insists on causing problems."

Paul walked to a large mirror on the side wall and motioned to it. "Might I remind you that this is a two-way mirror, behind which, at all session times, are anywhere from one to five doctors or student doctors." Paul walked back to his desk, rubbing his head.

Two student doctors watched Paul and Clare Benson through the observation mirror. The older student said, "Bite your tongue, Dr. Brandon. Don't say what you're thinking. Your other patients need you."

Paul was deep in thought, and Clare Benson was confused. "Dr. Brandon?" she asked.

"Yes," he responded.

"I like the teaching arrangement," she admitted. "Two or five heads are better than one. You see what a problem I have with my daughter."

Paul contemplated again.

The students continued to watch through the observation mirror. The younger student jumped to his feet. "Lady, your problem's not your daughter, it's your husband. And your daughter's problem is as much her mother as her stepfather!"

The older student stood up and patted his friend's shoulder. "But that's something the daughter probably won't even start to realize until she's pushing thirty or forty."

Paul was deep in thought, and Clare Benson was frustrated.

"Are you listening to me?" she asked. "How can I get my daughter to stop causing fights at home?"

Paul looked directly at Benson. "Have you asked your husband to respect your daughter's privacy by not opening the doors to her room and bathroom when she's in there? Or have you considered reinstalling the privacy locks on the doors? Since they were removed."

Clare Benson was incensed. "Why, Harold doesn't mean anything when he does that. He just likes to check on her. He certainly should be able to do that."

Paul was stunned as she continued. "He's a good husband and provider. What I need to know is what to do about that girl!"

Paul took a deep breath. "Solving this problem, the way it should be, will take time. And there isn't any time to waste."

"I agree," she quickly responded.

Paul rubbed his forehead. "Considering the whole situation, I think what needs to happen is for you to send your daughter to a nice, safe boarding school. Immediately. Since you can easily afford it. Meanwhile, we can work on a resolution. We have a lot to discuss and do."

Clare Benson got excited. "That would solve the fighting. But I don't know. Harold doesn't like it when she's not home. He shows such concern."

"Talk to Harold tonight and call me tomorrow. If necessary, I'll talk to Harold. You must get your daughter out of the house as soon as possible," Paul said.

Benson was thrilled. "This is a wonderful solution."

"This is not a solution. This is only a temporary measure that must be taken until we can reach a solution," Paul said emphatically. "We have a lot to do." Paul stood up, and so did Mrs. Benson. "Please do all you can to arrange things quickly for the boarding school as soon as possible." Paul walked Clare Benson to the door, and they said their goodbyes.

The students were still observing behind the mirror. The younger one said, "That's the quickest solution for this girl's safety. I never would have thought of that. This guy's a genius."

The older one responded, "Yep. Listen and learn. He's super sharp, smart, and creative."

Clare Benson left, and Paul closed the door. *Triple UGH!* he thought.

Chapter Two

Trust Is Priceless

There was a knock at his office door, and Paul opened it. It was Becky, trying to look pretty. "A Miss Hillerman called. She said to tell you she's in the lounge down the hall and to please come when you can."

Paul looked at Becky. "Thank you. And when I don't have a patient, it is perfectly appropriate to use the intercom," Paul instructed.

"Oh, I get a bit antsy and prefer not to sit so much," Becky responded. "I'd much rather move around." Then she reached toward Paul's mouth, but Paul moved away. "I thought there was something on your lip," she said.

Paul was irritated and paused. “The intercom works well. I'll be down the hall,” he said and quickly headed toward the reception room door.

Intercom, phewy! I like to move, and I like seeing you, she thought about Dr. Brandon.

Becky called after him. “Is Miss Hillerman your fiancée?”

“No, Miss Perkins,” Paul responded, trying not to be rude.

Becky was relieved. She ran a few steps and stopped. “Oh,” Becky added. “She said to knock twice, pause, and knock again. She has the door locked.”

Paul was bewildered but knocked as instructed. Paul and Loni had been good friends since they were in college, and she had dated Paul’s younger cousin for many years. Loni opened the door. She was a pretty woman in her mid-thirties. Her shoes were off, and her eyes were red and swollen from crying. She hugged Paul.

“I’m sorry to barge in like this, but I’m desperate. Thanks for coming,” she said between sniffles.

Paul entered the lounge, and Loni locked the door behind him. She picked up the bottle of wine off the table and started to pace.

Paul was seriously concerned. “Loni, what's the matter?”

“I had to see you. I had to remind myself that there is such a rare creature as a decent human being, especially a male," Loni said with a scowl.

"What's going on?" Paul asked.

"I'm getting plastered. Want to join me?" she replied.

Paul took the wine bottle and placed it back on the table. He gently led Loni to sit down on the couch. He sat next to her.

"Alcohol never solves any problem. Why aren't you at school? Who's with all those tiny kindergarteners?" Paul asked.

"Well, I don't know. Maybe Mr. Barker."

"The principal?"

Loni shrugged her shoulders. "You see, I've been given a two-week leave of absence. To get my head straight," she said sarcastically.

"Why?" Paul asked with deep concern.

"Do you remember that little girl, Erica, I helped in the bathroom? She had marks on her bottom and thighs from her father spanking her abusively. It looked as if he had used a belt or strap on a little kindergartener. Which should never be used on anybody!"

"Yes, it was awful. You are supposed to go to court to testify next month."

Loni ran her hand across her forehead. "Oh, there will be no court. There will be no action whatsoever. Her mother has seen to that! Her mother, who is supposed to care about her more than anyone. Can you believe that?"

"What? What happened?"

"It seems her mother is good friends with the district attorney and the head of the Board of Education." Loni sarcastically waved her hand. "Erica's parents are such good, upstanding people that it's unthinkable that anything improper could be going on!" Loni shook her head and breathed a huge sigh. "And they've brainwashed Erica to believe that I'm the enemy; I'm trying to destroy her family. She hates me."

"She's young and confused," Paul said. "She needs her parents to survive right now. I know that's got to be infuriating. But try not to take it personally. And, believe me, I know that's easier for me to say than for you to do."

"Infuriating, for sure! Erica told me her mother knew. She told me," Loni screamed. "But I couldn't believe it. Her mother! Not a stepmother or adopted mother. Not an aunt, or caretaker, or neighbor. Her own mother!" Loni cried uncontrollably, and Paul comforted her.

The hospital was quiet. Penny was in bed and still unconscious. Her green eyes were open but unseeing. She had a blank stare that required drops regularly placed into her eyes. The doctors had considered taping her eyes shut, but that was quickly ruled out to avoid further trauma should she regain consciousness. Her once ruddy cheeks were now colorless. Penny's sun-streaked, blonde hair fell in beautiful, natural curls resting on her white pillow.

Nurse Schmidt stroked Penny's head as Nurse Davis changed the IV bag.

"Do you think she's going to make it?" Nurse Schmidt asked with tears in her eyes.

Nurse Davis frowned. "It's not looking good. Don't get attached."

Loni had composed herself and was still explaining the situation to Paul in the lounge.

"Erica's been transferred out of my class, and the D.A. made it abundantly clear that I don't have a case. The whole time Erica's mother sat there grinning," Loni said through gritted teeth.

"What about the school nurse? Couldn't she confirm what you were saying?" Paul asked.

"Suddenly, she can't remember a thing, and all the written reports and drawings have magically disappeared. Even the paperwork from Social Services is all gone. It's worse than a horror movie," Loni said.

"I'll help you. We can do something," Paul encouraged.

"What? The principal glared at me. They also said if I try to pursue this problem-making, they will simply discredit me by bringing up the Caldwell case." Loni sighed, and tried not to cry.

"What's that?" Paul was puzzled.

"It was a different physical abuse case I was involved in years ago. I never told you about it. It seemed like an easy win. Then, when everything went wrong, I was embarrassed that I had been so naïve and stupid. I was the teacher who pushed for it to go to trial. I felt so bad for the kid. He was only six and had marks, scrapes, and bruises all over, and all the time. And occasionally he had burns. The attorney warned me it would take more evidence than we had. We needed witness testimony. But back then, I believed in the justice system. I was sure we would win and get him some help. He really needed it.

"They had excuses for every injury. He was clumsy. His friend knocked him down. He tripped. He fell down the steps. Unfortunately, the lawyer was right. The entire case was thrown out for lack of evidence. Just like that. Done. Over. So, the principal made it quite clear today that they'll say I've got a problem."

"Whoa. That is not good," Paul admitted.

"I don't know who to hate more—Erica's mother or the school nurse."

There was a knock at the door. "Dr. Brandon?" a voice called.

Paul patted Loni's arm and then answered the door. "Yes?" It was Becky.

"A Mrs. Klein is here for her appointment," Becky

said, and tried to flash a flirty smile.

"Thank you. Please tell her I'll be there soon," Paul replied.

Paul closed the door, and Loni stood up. "You go on. I'll be fine," Loni said.

"I'm not leaving you here to drown your sorrows. You know full well that alcohol only causes more problems. It never solves them. Watching your older sister struggle through AA should have taught you that. I want you to come to the office and wait for me in the reception area," Paul responded.

Loni smiled. "I'm a mess, and I just want to be alone. I'm going to take a nap. I'm exhausted." She yawned. "I do feel better after talking about this garbage. Like you always say, 'Talking helps.' And it does."

"Are you sure?" Paul asked.

"Yes, positive. Go. And I'll do no more drinking. I promise." Loni motioned with her hand. "After my nap, I may even order a pizza."

"You're sure?" Paul asked with his charming smile.

Loni giggled. "Positive. Now go," she insisted.

"You are a brave woman, Loni. Not many teachers will stand up for what's right. It's much easier to look the other way or ignore the problem and the truth. All the kids are lucky to have you. I'll be back as soon as I can." Paul kissed the top of Loni's head and picked up the bottle of wine. "And I'll take this with me, so you are not tempted again."

Loni laughed. "Smart idea. Thanks for caring."

After Paul left, Loni locked the door and thought, *Good friends and good people truly are priceless. Even if the rest of the world stinks.*

Chapter Three

Some Nightmares Become Reality!

Paul made a quick stop in the men's bathroom to pour the wine down the drain and throw the bottle in the trash. He straightened his tie.

As Paul entered the reception area, Marcy Klein was icy and harsh. She had a problem with one foot that caused her to limp slightly.

"I'm glad to meet you, Mrs. Klein. I'm Dr. Brandon."

Marcy Klein immediately recoiled. "There must be some mistake. I specifically requested a female doctor!"

"Please, step into my office. We'll get everything straightened out. I'm certain Dr. Ramsey will be happy to see you. She is terrific." Paul motioned the way.

Hesitantly, Marcy walked to Paul's office and entered.

Paul stopped at Becky's desk. “Does Dr. Ramsey have a patient scheduled?”

“Yeah, she does. Don't move,” Becky said in an uncharacteristic stern manner. Paul was startled as Becky picked something off his jacket sleeve. “This piece of fuzz was just hanging there,” she said as Paul backed away.

“Stop,” Paul hesitated and took a deep breath. He knew he needed to get back to Mrs. Klein. “When is the first available appointment for Dr. Ramsey?” Paul asked.

Becky looked at the calendar. “Tuesday at three,” she responded.

“Thank you,” Paul said and entered his office.

“Dr. Ramsey will be happy to work with you, but currently she has a patient. I'm sorry about the mix-up. We can get you scheduled for next Tuesday.”

Marcy Klein was irate. “Next week! I'm here now. It's not my fault the idiot I talked to scheduled me with a man.”

“I'm sorry for the inconvenience, and your first session will be at no charge. Could I get you a soda or a flavored water?” Paul asked.

Marcy was slightly surprised by the friendly gesture. “No, thank you.”

“Do you work around here?”

“No, it's a good distance from here,” Marcy answered uncomfortably.

"What kind of work do you do?" Paul asked.

Klein shifted in her seat. "Law. I am very close to taking the bar."

"What an accomplishment. Congratulations," Paul said with a smile.

Marcy Klein was extremely bitter and rash. "Accomplishment is right. I've worked seven days a week, fifty-two weeks a year, but I've done it! All by myself."

Paul's eyes widened. "You must enjoy law."

Klein seemed to soften slightly. "Actually, I plan to enter politics one day."

Becky sat at her desk in the reception area and filed her nails. She was oblivious to anything else that transpired. Carl Denton entered and walked to her desk with a scowl. He said gruffly, "I'm Dr. Denton, the hospital administrator of St. John's Memorial Hospital next door. You may have taken the large, enclosed glass-lined skybridge walkway between the two buildings for easier access, day or night. It connects the two buildings for convenient entrance and time savings."

Immediately, Becky sat up straight and attempted to hide her nail file. "I've seen it, but I've never walked across there. It's a little too high up for me," Becky admitted. “I like the elevator.”

Denton continued, “I know Dr. Ramsey's giving a lecture at seven thirty tonight, but how many appointments do she and Dr. Brandon have left for today?”

“After this, Dr. Ramsey has one, and Dr. Brandon has two,” she replied nervously.

Loni walked in and sat down, waiting for Dr. Denton to finish.

“As soon as they can, have them come to my office. Tell them it's urgent,” Denton instructed and rushed out.

Loni watched Carl leave and then walked to Becky with a note in her hand. “Please give this to Dr. Brandon.”

“Sure,” Becky responded and took the paper.

“Thanks,” Loni replied and walked toward the elevator.

“Hey,” Becky called, “that Dr. Brandon is a pretty all right guy, isn't he?”

Loni chuckled and stopped. “Oh, yes. He's great.” She thought for a moment and stepped back toward Becky. “He’s always honest with people and himself. And he's strong.”

Becky grinned. “I know. What a hunk.”

Loni shook her head. “No. I don't mean physically; I mean his character, his soul. Paul's not out to prove anything or impress anyone. He's just himself.”

Becky giggled and waved her hands. “Well, that's a good self to be.”

Loni smiled and took a step closer. "I think it's pathetic when guys try to be macho. They have no idea what it truly means to be a 'real man.'"

Becky nodded her head and leaned closer. "Boy, do I know what you mean."

Loni put her finger to her cheek. "You know, Paul's like some of the men you see on those old late-night movies."

"And dream about meeting," Becky added, putting her right hand on her chest. "But as they say, 'They don't make 'em like they used to.'"

"There are still some good guys around," Loni declared. "You just need to look for them. Well, see you." Loni walked toward the elevator.

Becky called to her. "Wait. Are you two dating?"

Loni stopped and turned back to Becky. "Paul? No. He's a great friend. But that wouldn't be hard to change." Loni grinned and left.

"Well, don't change it," Becky muttered quietly.

Paul opened his office door, and Mrs. Klein exited. She turned back to Paul and cracked a slight smile. "You're not that bad to talk to."

"Well, thank you." Paul nodded in his humble manner.

"I'll check my schedule and call for an appointment with Dr. Ramsey," she said.

"That's fine. Again, sorry about the mix-up. Good luck on the bar exam."

"Thanks."

Marcy Klein left, and Paul went to Becky's desk. "When Mrs. Klein comes in next week to see Dr. Ramsey, please give the bill to me."

"Okay," Becky said and handed Paul Loni's note. "I was asked to give you this. And Dr. Denton wants you and Dr. Ramsey in his office ASAP. It's important. He said it's urgent and for each of you to come after your last sessions."

"Okay. When Bridgett Morris arrives, please have her come in immediately. And under no circumstances are we to be disturbed." Paul stopped in his doorway, reading Loni's note to himself, as Judith walked up to Becky.

Paul, I'm fine. I'll call later. Love, Loni - P.S. Thanks for always being there.

Becky explained to Judith that Dr. Denton wanted to see them as soon as possible.

Paul started to enter his office, but Judith stopped him. "Paul, wait." She walked to Paul. "Do you know what Denton wants?"

"No idea. But I'm very close to a breakthrough with my next patient. I may run late."

"Lucky you." Judith smiled.

Bridgett Morris entered the reception area as the phone rang. Becky answered it. Paul was still standing in his doorway and saw her.

"Mrs. Morris, please come in," Paul said in his welcoming manner.

"I'll explain to Denton," Judith said.

"Thanks." Paul waited for Bridgett Morris. She entered his office. Paul followed and closed the door.

Becky turned to Judith. "That was Gloria Logan on the phone. She's sick and had to cancel."

"Then I'm going to Dr. Denton's office now," Judith said and headed down the hall.

Carl Denton, other doctors, and nurses were talking in the hall. Carl saw Judith and rapidly walked to meet her.

"That was fast," Carl grinned.

"I had a cancellation, but Paul has his appointment," Judith responded.

"Great that you had a cancellation. I'm sorry Paul didn't too. I wanted to talk to both of you together, but let's get started. This is crucial. We can fill Paul in later." Carl rushed Judith toward his office. "Please, in here. What a day."

Judith joined Carl in his office. "Sit down, please. I need your help. And Paul's." Judith sat down, looking somewhat bewildered.

"These visiting psychiatrists can't solve a crossword

puzzle, much less an emotional nightmare. I can't wait until they're all gone. The whole lot of them."

Judith was puzzled. "What's up?"

"There's an eight-year-old girl who hasn't spoken a word or done anything in over two months." Carl looked seriously at Judith. "She won't eat. She won't drink. She won't move. Nothing. That's why she was admitted. She is literally starving to death. I.V.s can only do so much. She's wasting away!"

"What's wrong with her?" Judith asked with genuine concern.

"At first, we thought it was shock, but it's way more than that." Carl rubbed his face with both hands.

"What's happened? Why is she so bad?" Judith inquired.

Carl looked seriously at Judith. "She's given up the will to live. We're feeding her intravenously, but it takes more than calories to keep a person alive. She needs help. And quickly!"

Paul was sitting patiently, waiting for his client to respond. She was in obvious distress but was debating whether to admit the truth of what had happened. She looked at the floor and then at Dr. Brandon.

"If I tell you everything, will you stop seeing me as a patient?" She did not wait for a reply but kept talking.

"It's hard to admit stuff to you, but I couldn't stand the thought of not having you to talk to." She finally paused.

Paul offered her comforting and understanding advice. "Mrs. Morris, we are in this together. I am here to help you verbalize some of the hard parts, not abandon you when you need help. I am right here and not going anywhere."

"That's good to know. Truthfully, I am an awful person, and I've been afraid to tell you about everything, as I think you've been suspecting for a while. I don't think I would even want to be my friend. I've been trying to change this whole mess, but nothing has worked," Bridgett said and started to cry.

"You know," Paul said gently, "it is a good sign that you are experiencing such remorse and regret. Many people rarely display or have those responses. They are only glad they were never caught. Rarely do some people ever feel remorse about those they've hurt or the awful things they've instigated. It may not seem like it, but you are in a much more favorable place than those with no bad feelings or regrets."

"Really?" Bridgett asked in hope.

"Really," Paul assured her.

"Well, I can't keep living with this guilt, that's for sure! Most of the time, I feel like I'm about to lose it!" Bridgett looked at Paul and took a deep breath. "I've been cheating on my husband for almost five months now, and I don't know how to get out of it. At this point,

I feel trapped. I don't know what to do.

"I've been helping a long-time friend of my older brother, John. His friend, Kirk, was severely injured skiing. Kirk is six years older than I am. He's way cute, and originally, it was quite flattering. Once upon a time, I had a huge crush on him. But I never meant for any of this to happen."

Bridgett looked at Paul, expecting fiery darts to come her way. "So, what has transpired?" Paul asked in his gentle manner.

"At first, I was just helping him with his extensive injuries and strengthening exercises. Then, one day, out of the blue, he kissed me. It was like a fairytale that had come true. As I said, I had had a crush on him for years when I was younger. It was exciting, and I didn't know what to do. So, I did nothing, and it happened again and then again! Nothing ever happened but kissing. I realized quickly that it was just a childhood fantasy, and I was not in love with him. I really do love my husband. But I feel trapped. I don't want to hurt my brother or Kirk, especially since he's still recuperating. And I know for sure my husband will not understand. A big part of our relationship has always been built on trust. And, boy did I blow that!"

Bridgett looked earnestly at Paul. "You know I always tell you to tell it to me straight and not sugarcoat anything. Right?"

Paul chuckled. "Yes. You are excellent regarding

wanting the truth and getting straight to the point. I admire that." He looked directly at Bridgett. "So, let's consider some facts. You know, your brother's friend was probably very vulnerable because of his injuries. Often, when people are recuperating or sick, they react in ways they would never have otherwise. He is probably on some pain medication, as well."

"Absolutely. You are right, and I appreciate it when you tell me things candidly. It drives me nuts when people beat around the bush. Please continue," Bridgett said.

"Well, we are trained to go slowly so people reach the right conclusions and voluntarily make changes. But, since you prefer a more direct approach, I work a bit differently with you."

Paul looked at Bridgett. "Don't you think Kirk would have asked you out before the accident and before you were married if he had wanted to date you? I know at one point you would have been too young for him, but not as you got older. But it is my understanding, he never did ask you out."

"No. Never." Bridgett listened intently. She hung on Paul's every word as he continued.

"It is also great and vitally important that you recognize you truly love your husband. That is crucial and very beneficial. You have been helping Kirk at an extremely vulnerable time. With his injuries, he is not completely himself.

"I believe wholeheartedly that people should see and grasp the whole and clear truth. Do you think that you are overestimating your importance regarding Kirk's life and recovery? And possibly underestimating your husband's understanding and ability to forgive? You said that nothing ever happened other than kissing. That is huge information for any husband."

Bridgett was soaking in every word and thought. "Please, tell me more!" she pleaded.

"It is possible that your caring heart is keeping you trapped. I know it's hard to walk away from those who need help. But maybe it's time to let the rehab staff take over completely for you before you ruin your marriage, not even intending for that to happen. And maybe it's time for you to allow your husband the opportunity to prove how much he does love you, and that he can forgive.

"Not everyone has that deep love or forgiveness inside of themselves. But your husband seems terrific, and possibly he does have that capability."

Paul looked straight into Bridgett's eyes. He asked, "So, what real ability for loving and forgiving do you think your husband has?"

Bridgett bit her lip and smiled. She thought silently and deeply. "Listening to you gives me hope. My husband is incredible." She pondered for several minutes. "I do think he loves me enough to forgive me! Especially since I never meant for any of this to happen." Bridgett cried tears of joy and relief. Paul was thankful for her awareness.

"And you are absolutely right, Dr. Brandon. If Kirk had been interested in me, he had years of opportunity to ask me out before I was married. I don't even need to feel bad at all. Let the professionals help him. You are saving me, Dr. B, and my marriage! A thousand-pound weight just lifted off me!"

"Guilt can be a pretty heavy burden to carry at times," Paul said.

"I can't believe it. I can even breathe better. I will wish Kirk well, pat him on the head, and say goodbye. But first, I'm going home to my wonderful husband. This is the first time I've wanted to go home in ages. I've been too scared of getting caught or smothering in guilt."

Paul smiled. "Those are all great choices."

"You are terrific! I love you, Dr. B. In the right way." Bridgett smiled and jumped up. "I can't wait to see my husband and come clean."

"It's okay. Go. We can end early," he encouraged her.

"Thanks. You are the best." Bridgett hurried out of the office. Then she turned around and ran back into the office, giving Paul a big hug. "That's an okay kind of hug," she said, and hurried down the hall, with hope in her every step.

Well, that was one potential disaster avoided, Paul thought and smiled.

Chapter Four

Reliving Past Horrors Keeps You Stuck

Carl and Judith were still mulling over Penny's situation. They were both heartsick over her plight and aching to help. Judith stood quietly in the corner of Penny's hospital room and observed. Then she motioned to Carl for them to leave and put her hand to her mouth in desperation.

"Let's go to my office," Carl quietly suggested. He turned to Penny. "I'll be back shortly, little one," Carl said and patted her shoulder.

Paul's patient, Amy O'Connor, finally responded.

Amy spoke quietly. “You'll think I'm bad,” she said, as tears filled her eyes.

“No. I think you've been hurt, and it will help tremendously if you talk about it. We’ve been through a lot together to get to where we are. You said you'd let me help you face it. You can do this. It will help you feel much better to release all you’ve been hiding. Don't fight it, let it go,” Paul encouraged.

Amy looked at Paul. She wiped the tears that streamed down her cheeks. She took a deep breath and burst out.

“It was my grandfather. The first time I can remember, I was about five years old. It never stopped until he died when I was eleven.” Amy rubbed her hands together and swallowed several times.

“Every Sunday morning, he would stay in bed, and they would send me up to ‘spend time’ with him. I didn't see much of him during the week because he worked a lot.” Amy stopped talking and sobbed.

After waiting in silence, Paul took the tissue box from his desk and held it toward Amy. She rapidly took four tissues from the box and blew her nose.

Paul waited a long moment and asked, “Who would send you upstairs?”

Amy took a deep breath. “Usually, my grandmother. Sometimes my mother. We lived with my grandparents after my mom got divorced.” Amy looked at Paul.

“As I got older, I wondered what the two of them were

doing while I was upstairs," she said in utter anguish. "It seems like they must have known what was going on."

Judith and Carl were seated in his office. Carl looked at Judith in frustration. "I'll tell you what I do know about Penny. Her father apparently ran off for a few weeks. Then late one night, he returned home and declared that he'd found religion." Carl lifted his hands and shook his head.

"Found religion?" Judith asked, completely confused.

"Yes. He proceeded to get the children, Penny and her six-year-old brother, Ben, out of their beds and take them into the kitchen."

Judith listened intently.

"He told them he was going to teach them a life lesson."

Judith grimaced fiercely.

"At gunpoint, he told his wife to lie on the floor. The jerk told the children to sit one on each side of the mother."

"What?" Judith exclaimed.

Carl shook his head and continued. "Next, while unbuttoning his shirt, he preached a sermon on how God made woman for man and made them a couple. Need I say more?"

"You've got ..." Judith started to interrupt, but she stopped herself.

Carl continued. "Oh, and he told the children not to move; if they did, he'd shoot them. They weren't to blink their eyes or make a sound."

The hospital hallway was bustling. A nurse handed a form on a clipboard to a brash, young doctor. The doctor rudely grabbed it. "I'm not signing anything. I'll get Dr. Denton to sign."

The doctor walked to Denton's office and opened the door. "Sorry to interrupt, but …"

"Not now. You handle it," Dr. Denton said firmly.

The doctor closed the door, and Carl turned back to Judith.

"Sparing you details, the father became preoccupied, and the gun was on the floor." Carl raised an eyebrow. "The six-year-old, Ben, got the gun, held it with both hands, and blew his father's brains out. Smart kid, eh? I, myself, consider him a child prodigy."

"Oh, no! Those poor children," Judith shrieked.

Carl rubbed his chin as tears filled his eyes. "The angle of the shot splattered Penny literally from head to toe. Covered with blood and flesh from her father." Carl gestured down his body. "That's how she was found. Still sitting Indian-style, and she hasn't done a thing since. The EMTs gently straightened out her legs when they placed her on the gurney to take her out of the house. Thankfully, a neighbor heard the shot and called the police."

"That poor child. Both of them!" Judith said aghast, placing her hands on her cheeks.

"Now, ask me how I know so well what happened," Carl said with clenched fists.

Judith motioned for Carl to continue.

"This Bozo recorded the whole thing," Carl explained with disgust. "I have a copy of the video that was taken on his phone. He positioned it to capture everything."

Judith's eyes got big. She was stunned, and her mouth dropped in disbelief.

"Shocked?" Carl asked, and Judith was speechless.

"That's not the worst," Carl continued. "The father had done things like this for years. The landlady had begged the mother to leave him, but she wouldn't."

"Unbelievable!" Judith exclaimed with outrage.

"There's more," Carl stated. "The mother's furious with Ben for having shot her husband and furious with Penny for not stopping Ben."

"The mother's crazier than the father. If that's possible," Judith stated emphatically.

"The mother also yelled at Penny while she was sitting on the floor, covered with blood and flesh, in a state of shock, that nothing Penny could ever do or say would make her forgive her." Carl looked firmly at Judith. “Obviously, that plays a big part in Penny's near comatose state. It's a shame Ben didn't shoot the mother too!” Carl closed his eyes and rubbed his temples.

Judith’s mouth was agape. She sat in silence, then finally managed some words. “Carl, this is beyond horrific. How's Ben?”

“Surprisingly, Ben seems fine. He's in a good, loving foster home. A family I know personally. After talking to the neighbors, social services took the children from the mother.”

“Why didn't one of those neighbors call and get help for these children long ago?” Judith asked rhetorically.

“Tell me about it. I'm sick of hearing, ‘If we had only known it would come to this’ or ‘I didn't think it was any of our business!’”

Judith’s anger soared. “Mistreated children are everybody's business. And if more people would speak up, a lot of this trash would stop.”

Carl nodded. “If a dog is mistreated, five out of ten people will do something. Maybe even more than five. But if a child’s in trouble, most people won't get involved,” Carl said in complete frustration.

“I hope we can help,” Judith sighed.

“So, do I. If Penny isn't reached, she's going to die,” Carl reluctantly admitted.

Paul and Amy O'Connor paused at Paul's office door before opening it. Amy looked and felt much better. She smiled at Paul.

"It helped me so much when you explained that I was never bad. I was always a victim in this nightmare. All the guilt I've carried for years seems to have melted away. Thank you for that. I'm going straight home and start your plan," Amy committed.

"I am so glad the truth has freed you from that unwarranted guilt. And an excellent choice, get started immediately. Writing things down helps to get everything that's buried out in the open. Just a spiral notebook and a pen can do wonders. Putting things down on paper helps you not to hold on to them and carry them everywhere you go. Acknowledge the pain in the notebook and close the cover. You can revisit it when you are ready and want to, instead of having to deal with it constantly. It takes time, but it works. It's a great step toward freedom from past garbage. Call anytime you need or want to," Paul advised.

"Thank you. I'll see you next week," Amy said with a huge sigh.

"Before, if necessary," Paul responded. "You were very courageous today."

Amy smiled and fought back tears. "Thank you. You always help a lot. See ya." She opened the door and walked down the hall, beaming with every step.

Becky walked over to Paul. "Dr. Ramsey's last appointment canceled. She already went to Dr. Denton's office," she told him.

"Great. I'm headed there now," Paul replied.

Becky looked at Paul and walked closer to him. "Dr. Brandon, I need your help," she said.

"What's the problem?" Paul asked.

"I'm going to the spa from here. I need to change, but, well, my zipper got stuck," she stammered and turned her back to Paul. Becky moved her hair to the side, out of the way.

Paul was irritated, but Becky grinned in ecstasy. He forced the zipper upward.

"Miss Perkins, I suggest you wait until after business hours to tend to personal matters. I would appreciate more professional conduct in the office. Thank you. Please forward any emergency calls to my pager," Paul stated emphatically.

Becky's disappointment and frustration were apparent. Paul hurriedly left, and Becky stormed to her desk.

Judith and Carl stood beside Penny's hospital bed, watching her lie unmoving, her eyes staring blankly. Penny was very frail. Carl gently patted Penny's hand. He was going to introduce Penny to Judith this time.

"Penny, there's someone here I want you to meet. This is a friend of mine, Dr. Ramsey. She wants to help you." Carl looked at Judith.

"Hello, Penny. You sure have pretty hair."

Penny showed no response. Judith looked at Carl and back at Penny.

"I'm going to check your eyes," Carl said to the little girl, "and you tell me if the light's too bright. Okay?"

Judith held her hand to her mouth. She was shocked to see how bad Penny's condition truly was.

Carl took the small flashlight from his pocket. He examined Penny's eyes. First one eye, then the other, then both eyes together. Judith talked to Penny as Carl examined her eyes.

"When I was a young girl, I liked to play with dolls and swing. But what I liked the most was climbing trees. What do you like to do?" Judith asked.

Judith waited, but there was no response or movement from Penny.

"I'm leaving now, so you can get some rest. I'll be back soon, and we can play some games." Judith walked somberly to the foot of the bed.

Carl bent over Penny and lovingly stroked her head. "Penny, Ben sends his love. He wants you to hurry up and feel better so you two can play together. I'll be back to check on you later."

Carl and Judith left Penny's room and entered the hall.

Judith put her hand to her temple and stared at Carl. “This is really bad,” Judith said, and shook her head. “There’s no other way to describe it.”

Carl respected Judith’s opinion immensely and was panic-stricken. He had seen Judith work miracles over the years, and that is what they needed now for Penny—a miracle. “How bad is it?” Carl asked with trepidation.

“I don't know the extent yet, but I can tell you this is a nightmare. Penny’s worse than I thought she was when I first saw her. It will take time to get a full assessment.”

Carl sighed deeply. “She doesn't have much time. You've got to work fast to have any hope of success.”

“I'll do my best,” Judith responded. “I want Paul to see her. He catches things faster than the rest of us. At times, it’s like he has an insight that we lack, especially with children.” Judith and Carl walked down the hall.

“Penny is now my top priority,” Judith reassured Carl. “I'll get back to you as soon as I can.”

“Thank you, Judith. I'll have that awful video set up in locked consult room two and get you a key,” Carl responded.

Judith was waiting for the elevator next to the nurses’ station. When the doors opened, Paul exited.

“Boy, am I glad you're here,” Judith said frantically.

"You look positively sick. Are you okay? What happened?" Paul asked as the elevator doors closed.

"Come with me. There's a video waiting for us to watch. After which, I'm sure, we'll both be sick," Judith replied.

Becky was seated at her reception desk, wearing her workout clothing while on the phone. "Anna, I can't believe it. Absolutely nothing. And after all the trouble you had getting my zipper stuck...."

Judith and Paul had just finished the video that showed everything regarding that horrible night, including Ben shooting his biological father. Paul handed Judith a box of tissues. She wiped her eyes and the tears from her cheeks, then blew her nose.

"Shooting was too good for him!" Judith said with her jaws clenched.

Paul was stunned and silently walked over to stop the video. "Seeing children abused is sickening. It is absolutely the worst! You can get used to accidents, illness, even death, but not child abuse," Paul admitted with anger and sadness.

"You are so right. Anyone who gets used to child

abuse should change fields. When you see her, Penny looks even more pathetic and helpless, motionless in her hospital bed. She breaks my heart," Judith said.

There was a knock at the door. Paul opened it, and a nurse entered.

"Dr. Ramsey, your husband is waiting downstairs. He said to remind you that you're giving a lecture tonight," the nurse said.

"Oh, thank you. I completely forgot about that," Judith responded.

"You're welcome," the nurse replied and closed the door as she left.

Judith looked at Paul. "I don't know if I should go. We need to spend every minute we have figuring out how to reach Penny," Judith said.

"Every moment counts, but you need to go to your seminar. Maybe reviewing those lecture notes will help you find some ideas," Paul suggested. "Plus, it's too late to cancel."

Judith shook her head in frustration. "I guess you're right. I've had lots of emergencies, but never this kind of pressure. Psychiatry and psychology are not fast-acting. It takes time. Time, we don't have. You'll see what I mean when you meet Penny," Judith sighed. "She's bad. Really bad."

Paul adamantly responded, "This can be fast. We have to find the right key to Penny's closed door." Paul contemplated and continued. "I think the fastest route is through the mother. It may not be the best, but the fastest."

Surprised, Judith responded, "That makes sense. But do you think she'll even help?"

"I don't know, but we need to try. I'm going to see Penny. If you think of anything, please call me," Paul said.

"Of course," Judith replied. "Tomorrow's your day to go to the schools, isn't it?"

Paul nodded.

"I can be here extra early in the morning. I'll get what I can regarding the mother. Leave me a list of what you find, so I don't waste time duplicating," Judith requested.

"We need to know all we can from the neighbors and the police report. I'll leave everything for you and Carl in an envelope addressed to you on Carl's desk. It's safest there," Paul said.

Judith smiled. "Thank you. Have Carl go with you to see Penny. He's very good with her."

After Judith left, Paul looked at the television screen and wrangled with his inner anger. *Those poor kids!* he thought. He scratched his head, stepped into the hall, and headed to Carl's office.

Carl's office was empty. Paul just stood and contemplated where he could find Carl. As the hospital administrator, he was often busy. He could have been anywhere in the building. As Paul was considering having Carl paged, Carl walked up and placed his hand on Paul's shoulder.

"I'm sure glad to see you. Come in. Any clues?" Carl asked as they entered his office. "Never mind. That's an unfair question so soon. But I have confidence that you and Judith can do this."

"I hope you're right," Paul admitted.

"My granddaughter is in a school play tonight, and I promised her I'd be there." Carl quickly gathered things from his desk. "Besides, if I don't show up, my wife will starch my underwear. Oh, I do hate that. But it certainly is effective."

Paul was perplexed. "Why would Glenda starch your underwear?"

Carl chuckled. "All these years, she's never complained, never yelled, or nagged. Nothing." Carl put on his coat and continued, "If I do something she doesn't like, or don't do something I should have, I end up with stiff boxers."

Paul cocked his head to the left and looked at Carl. "I don't get it."

"Years ago, when Glenda first started this, I asked her about it, and she said, 'If I have to be irritated, so do you.' She's a genius."

Paul and Carl both laughed, and Carl continued, "Brother, was she right. I was so irritated I could hardly sit. It sure has made me a considerate husband. The woman's brilliant."

Carl started to leave, but Paul stopped him. "Do you have time to go with me to Penny's room? I need to see her."

"Of course," Carl said, and grabbed his briefcase.

Carl and Paul entered Penny's room. She was still motionless. The nurses regularly had to turn and adjust her to prevent bedsores and apply her eye drops. Carl walked to Penny's bedside and stroked her head gently.

"How's my favorite patient? Ben said he's making you some pictures." Carl gingerly patted Penny's head. "Penny, I brought another friend to meet you. I think you'll like him."

"Hi, Penny. I'm Dr. Brandon, Dr. Denton's friend. I hope I can be your friend too," Paul said. His eyes widened, and he gave Carl a shocked look.

Carl nodded to Paul and showed his desperation, then turned to Penny. "I need to leave now, Penny, but I'll be back to see you in the morning. Okay?" Carl patted the top of Penny's head.

Paul added, "I'll be back in just a few minutes. I know some good stories I think you'll like."

Penny had not moved at all. Paul shook his head as he and Carl left the room.

Almost in a whisper, Paul said, "Carl, she is worse than I thought she'd be. I'm scheduled to be at the different high schools tomorrow."

"Oh, that experimental program you've been working on," Carl responded.

"Yes. Since I won't be here, I wanted to ask you, please come up with a nickname for Penny," Paul requested. Carl looked puzzled. "We need to establish a new and protected environment for Penny to feel safe enough to emerge, and a nickname may help with creating that. One that's not commonly used, so we're sure her father never called her by that name."

"That's a great idea." Carl flared his hand in excitement and hope. "Thank you for thinking of that. I've been desperate for something or some way to help," he replied sincerely, as he grasped Paul's arm. "I never would have thought of that."

Paul looked earnestly at Carl. "You're incredibly good with her, and that'll be an enormous help. Tonight, please think of an endearment, one that her father or mother could not possibly have used. Something unique."

Carl paused and thought. "I'll try," he agreed, letting go of Paul's arm.

"I want you to use the term you come up with often. Establish the word as yours and Penny's," Paul suggested.

"You mean like Pumpkin or Peaches, but something more unusual?" Carl asked.

"Exactly," Paul replied. "Something that will be

completely new for you to call her."

"Okay. I'll do it," Carl said.

"Penny looks much worse physically than I expected," Paul admitted.

"Like I told Judith, she's lost the 'will to live.' You don't hear much about it in med school or anywhere, for that matter. But it's real." Carl looked seriously at Paul. "I've seen a man live twenty-three years who shouldn't have lasted two weeks. And I saw a young widow in her thirties die when absolutely nothing was wrong with her."

Carl hesitated and then continued, "This is as immediate as it gets. Come by tomorrow after your school interviews. I'll wait, no matter how late it is."

"I'll see you then. Enjoy the play." Paul smiled, and Carl nodded as he left. Paul took a deep breath and entered Penny's room again.

The school auditorium seats were full. People were standing along the walls in the back. Various parents, grandparents, and family members were in the audience. Carl and Glenda were seated and holding hands. The narrator was offstage and said, "And the big bad wolf sneaked down the path . . .."

"Carl, are you all right?" Glenda asked.

"Yes, dear. I'm fine," Carl said.

"Are you hungry?" she asked.

"No," he replied.

"You keep mumbling about food: peaches, kiwi, raspberry," Glenda explained.

"Oh, I'm trying to think of a name." Carl chuckled.

"For what, a fruit salad?" Glenda smiled. Carl kissed her hand.

"I'll explain later," he whispered.

Still offstage, the narrator said, "Off they ran for their lives," while the children rushed across the stage to thunderous applause.

Chapter Five

Those Who Genuinely Care Are Rare

The sunrise was breathtakingly beautiful. Judith was not usually at the hospital this early in the morning and was struggling a bit as she pressed forward. While she exited the elevator, the sun's rays streamed through the windows, welcoming the coming of day. She did enjoy seeing that magnificent display Mother Nature provided. Judith walked by the nurses' station on her way to Carl's office.

"Good morning. I'm getting some info Dr. Brandon left for me in Dr. Denton's office," Judith said.

"Wow. You're here early. Dr. Brandon's still in there. He's been here all night," Nurse Roth replied.

"All night? Seriously?" Judith was shocked.

"Yeah. He went to the police station, but the rest of the time he's been in Dr. Denton's office or Penny Johnson's room," Nurse Roth explained.

"Thank you for the update," Judith said and headed to Carl's office.

Judith gently opened Carl's office door. His desk was a mess. There were papers spread all over it. Paul was asleep, with his head on the papers on the desk. Judith looked around the room and walked to Paul.

"Wake up, Paul. It's almost six thirty. You've been here all night," Judith said.

Paul awoke with a jolt and looked at his watch. "My alarm didn't go off."

"What is all this?" Judith asked.

Paul stretched and gathered the papers. "It's the police reports and all my notes to you and Carl." Paul straightened his clothes and buttoned his collar. "We've got to have more details from the neighbors. Could you contact Michael Webster and have him get on that as soon as he can?"

"Is he the medical student you sometimes hire to do research?" Judith queried.

"Yes. He's incredibly good, thorough, and fast. Just what we need right now," Paul responded.

"Of course," Judith said, and took a thumb drive from her purse. "Would you have time to look at the video I told you about that we developed? It just came. I wish you had been here to help create it."

"Sure. Stick it in the computer," Paul responded.

Penny was unconscious in her hospital bed. Two interns were working on adjusting her necessary equipment. One fixed Penny's I.V., and the other reconnected her to the heart monitor.

"Man, she looks bad," Intern Dunn sighed.

"I know. I've never worked on such a hopeless-looking kid before," Intern Grimes replied, as his hands shook.

Judith stopped the video that was playing on the computer. "So, what did you think? Terrific, isn't it?" she asked Paul enthusiastically.

Paul looked at Judith and hesitated. He raised his eyebrows. "Well..." he responded hesitantly.

Judith gasped. "'Well?' You see a video I, and a whole staff of professionals, have been working on for six months, and your only comment is 'well!'"

Paul listened patiently with an understanding smile as Judith continued, "There are so few aids available to help teach children. Sexual abuse gets worse every year. These kids need help." Judith realized she had begun to rant before Paul had given his opinion. She paused. “I do go on, don't I?”

“Yes, but it's good for the soul.” Paul chuckled. “Even a vivacious one like yours.”

“Paul Brandon, you are wise and astute beyond your years. You're a special man and doctor,” Judith declared.

“Aaaawwww. Thanks. You're rather special yourself,” he offered with a smile.

Judith shook her finger at Paul. “I may be able to teach you technique, but you have an inner quality I have yet to identify. But I am going to figure you out eventually,” Judith declared.

“Oh, I'm sure you will. But I'll keep you guessing as long as I can,” Paul said and slyly grinned.

Judith's watch alarmed. She quickly stopped it. “We don’t have much time. Please tell me why you had such a reserved response?” Judith took a sip of her water.

“Disappointment, I guess,” Paul confessed.

“Disappoint.... No, I won't say a word. Go ahead. Please continue,” she said and took a deep breath.

Paul stood up and paced. “Judith, for what the video addresses, it's terrific.” Paul's disappointment and Judith's confusion were obvious. Paul continued, “It shows the need for children to beware of public school teachers, Sunday school teachers, scout masters (if there are any still around), and the nice old man down the street. Not to mention the nuns that visit when you're sick.”

Judith was confused. "If it's so good, why are you disappointed?"

Paul gestured as he spoke to Judith. "No one tells children what to do when their own father, father-figure, mother, or family member is the sexual abuser, or abusers, for that matter!" Judith looked seriously at Paul as he continued. "How many of our adult patients have much of their inability to deal with life, or enjoy it, stemming from sexual abuse as a child? And a big chunk of that abuse comes from an immediate family member, relative, friend, or neighbor that's close enough to be family.

"For decades, youth have learned about 'Stranger Danger,' but in reality, that is a small part of a big problem!"

Judith gasped. "You are right!" she responded. Then she shook her head and gave a sad look.

Paul checked the time. "I've got to run." He handed Judith a piece of paper. "Here's a list of schools and the times I'll be at each of them. Please call if you need me. Have you found the mother?" Paul asked.

"I called her last night. She's coming today at 12:30. She is cold. It's not going to be easy to get her to talk to Penny. I don't think she cares if Penny dies!" Judith declared with disgust.

"She must help. After watching the video again and reading the reports, I'm sure she's our fastest key to reaching Penny. Please tell Becky that if she hears from

Benson or O'Connor, she's to reach me immediately. Any other messages can wait," Paul stated.

"Got it. Benson and O'Connor," Judith repeated.

"Thanks. I've got to hurry," Paul said.

"But Paul, you look awful," Judith observed.

"I have a razor and disposable toothbrushes in the car. They should help some. Good luck with Mrs. Johnson," Paul said as he hurried out the door.

"I'll need it," Judith called.

Carl called Paul as he was driving to his first school. "Paul, I have not come up with anything good for a nickname. I'm just drawing a blank. Do you have any ideas whatsoever?" Carl asked in desperation.

"I'll do some thinking. And I am going to talk to Ben later. His foster home is not far from my first school. Maybe he can help us," Paul suggested.

"I sure hope so. I like your plan and want to get it started as soon as possible," Carl admitted.

"I'll get back to you," Paul said.

Paul decided to make a quick trip to see Ben before going to his first school. Penny's situation was desperate, and Paul wanted to get the nickname in use as soon as possible.

When Paul stopped by the foster parents' home to see Ben, he was quite taken by the little guy. Ben was adorable and exuded sweetness and innocence. He had blond curls like Penny and a smile that radiated joy and melted the hardest of hearts. Ben was full of energy, and his big brown eyes sparkled. His pudgy little hands and chubby cheeks warmed Paul inside and brought a chuckle. Ben was very happy that Paul wanted to talk about Penny. Every day, he missed her terribly.

"Hey, buddy," Paul said. "Do you think you could help me come up with a nickname that would be good for Penny? We need a name that will mean something to Penny. And it should be fun too. Oh, and one that's never been used before."

Paul sat on the floor and played cars with Ben as they talked. "Can Penny come home yet?" Ben asked.

"Not yet. But we're hoping a fun name for her might help her and get her home faster."

Paul's quick stop paid off. He called Carl from his car and left a message. "Carl, I already stopped to see Ben. What a cute kid he is. He makes you smile. Ben said that Penny has a scooter that she loves, and she is great at riding it. So, try using 'Scooter' as a nickname. This is only for you to call her. That's important.

"And for sure, nobody has ever called her that before. I asked Ben. And even though that may seem more like a boy's nickname, what we're doing is way more than just using a nickname. We're trying to create enough security and safety so that Penny will come out of hiding. Also important, she will only have good memories related to her scooter. Certainly, it's worth trying. Please start using it as soon as you can."

Paul could not stop thinking about Ben or Penny. Even though their eyes were different colors, they looked very much alike. He hoped one day to see Penny as joyous as Ben.

Carl was at the hospital early as well. After making some quick rounds, he quietly peeked into Penny's room and then entered.

"Good morning, Penny. Ben says you are great at riding your scooter and that you love riding it. That sounds like such a fun thing to do. How about I call you Scooter? Would that be okay with you?" Carl paused. There was no response.

"Look, I brought you the cutest stuffed doggy I could find." Carl gently wiggled the dog in front of Penny. "His name's Fido, but you can change it to whatever you want, Scooter. I got you a CD player and some CDs with fun kid music, too, Scooter. We can play . . .."

A nurse entered the room and interrupted Carl. "Here are the night reports you requested. There have been no changes, but she's lost another quarter pound."

"Ugh. Thank you," Carl said to the nurse and returned to Penny. "You sweet little Scooter, we've got to get some weight on you fast."

The nurse looked at Penny, then Carl, and smiled as she left.

Paul parked in his assigned spot at Grover Valley High School. He was having trouble concentrating on anything except how to help Penny. Reaching the designated area inside the building marked Guidance Counselors, Paul saw one of his favorite counselors, Billy Langford. Unfortunately, many counselors at the various schools Paul helped were only there for the paycheck and long summer vacations. Billy was different. He cared about the students and tried hard to help them, which Paul wished everyone would do. Paul had even gotten two counselors fired for their treatment of the teens.

"Good morning, Billy. Do you have any appointments for me today?" Paul asked.

"Yeah, I do, but you'd better check with Harman first. She's on one of her rampages." Paul opened his mouth to speak, but Billy continued, "I used to think she was a man-hater, but it's not just men; it's women, too. She hates all adults."

"What about the teens?" Paul asked.

"Ah, she's great with the kids. That's how she keeps her job. It's like night and day, Doc," Billy said.

Barbara Harman was often cold and stern with the adults at the school. No one dared call her by her first name. Harman entered the Guidance Counselor area and snapped at Paul. "You're late," she snarled.

"Yes. I'm sorry," Paul replied.

"I have a student coming in ten minutes to see you, and that doesn't give much time for her background and history." Harman walked toward her office, and Paul followed.

Billy cautiously stopped Paul and spoke softly. "See what I mean? Gestapo material. I bet she's got bamboo shoots in her top drawer." He gestured toward the counselor's desk.

Paul smiled and winked at Billy as he entered Harman's office and closed the door. Harman motioned for Paul to sit down in the chair, and he did.

Harman was still standing as she looked through the papers on her desk. "Katherine Renolds is having a problem accepting that her sister has gone elsewhere to live." Harman sat down behind her desk. "I have been of no help. Frankly, I have a difficult time accepting the situation myself."

"What is it?" Paul asked.

Harman sighed deeply. "When Katherine's father drinks, he tries to force himself on one of his daughters," she said with disgust. "He kisses them on the lips, slobbering and falling all over them and saying, 'Give Daddy a good night kiss.'"

"Where's the mother?"

"This is in front of the mother and the other children. Who knows what goes on in private?"

Paul was shocked, and he scowled.

Harman continued, "The father hasn't bothered Katherine yet, and I stress, yet! Katherine's three older sisters have each been his prey."

"What's happened?" Paul inquired.

"The same pattern for all three. Shortly after this activity begins, the mother arranges for the victim, her daughter, to live elsewhere. The mother pays for the room and board and goes to visit her daughters, but they never return home. Katherine says she isn't sure if her mother ships the girls off for their safety or because she's jealous," Harman said with revulsion.

"Poor kid," Paul responded.

"It's baffling. The mother works and supports the husband. He only works part-time," Harman explained.

"But the mother stays with him?" Paul asked, aghast.

"Definitely. When the two oldest sisters left, it didn't affect Katherine that much. She wasn't close to them. But she and Babbs are extremely close." Harman stood and looked out of the window. "Also, she knows it's just a matter of time until her father confronts her." Harman looked directly at Paul. "Living under that ticking time bomb is taking a huge toll." Harman handed Paul a stack of papers.

Carl was still working with Penny. He had the CD player hooked up and was playing the Hokey Pokey song. Carl held Penny's hands and did the movements.

"Now, Scooter, we need to put our right hand in. We take our right hand out. We put our right hand in and shake it all about."

Carl wiggled the stuffed dog in front of Penny in a dancing motion. "Do you think this puppy likes to do the Hokey Pokey, Scooter?"

Nurse Schmidt entered the room. "The lab reports are back," she said, handing Carl papers.

Carl took the pages and handed the dog to the nurse. "Your turn to Hokey Pokey." Carl smiled.

Paul was still in Harman's office. "That's quite a history and a nightmare," Paul said, shaking his head in dismay.

"Katherine can't understand why her mother stays with him. The mother says the brothers need a father, but Katherine feels she and her sisters should count too. Frankly, so do I," Harman said as she squeezed her pen.

"Have you suggested to Katherine that she and

Babbs be placed in a foster home together?" Paul asked.

"The foster home is out. The mother earns a large salary and a commission, which is a problem. It provides her with plenty of resources to send her daughters away, at will. And Babbs enjoys being on her own in the rented room her mother found and provides for her, especially since she has no one to answer to. Harman brushed her jacket sleeve. "So did her two older sisters. They both ended up pregnant," Harman said with a sigh of despair.

"The girls are trying to make a family," Paul surmised.

"Yeah. One married an army private who wasn't the baby's father. The other sister married the baby's father after the baby was born. These poor girls." Harman paused and stifled her emotions.

"I'm not surprised," Paul admitted.

"The two older sisters have moved away. Katherine is convinced that Babbs will leave her, too, which makes all of this even harder," Harman explained.

"She's right. Those girls thought they liked being on their own, but those pregnancies were no accident," Paul declared.

The bell rang, and Harman looked at the clock. "Katherine is late. That's not like her." Harman pushed the intercom on her phone. "Is Katherine Renolds absent today?" Harmon asked.

"Yes, she is," the school secretary replied.

"Well, send Nancy Powell into Vice Principal Wick's office. He's out today," Harman instructed. "And give Katherine a call to check on her."

Harman looked sternly at Paul. "Katherine must be very sick; she hates staying home. Anyway, I want you to see Nancy."

"What's her background?" Paul asked.

"She claims nothing's wrong. But Nancy's gone from being an attractive, straight-A student to a creature who more resembles a 'bag lady' than a teenager," Harman said.

"That's a bad sign," Paul assessed.

"She's barely passing, but she won't tell me a thing. I hope she'll talk to you," Harman said.

"Me too. Please tell Billy I'm in Wick's office," Paul requested.

Nancy was pacing and biting her nails in Mr. Wick's office. She pulled at her long, plain skirt and knee socks. She tried to hide her bloody, nail-bitten fingers in the pockets of her bulky sweater. Paul knocked on the door and entered, startling Nancy.

"Hello, I'm Dr. Brandon. You must be Nancy?"

Paul offered his hand to Nancy. She reluctantly and timidly shook it.

"I like shaking hands. People tend to have a fear of

doctors, and I like to prove that I don't bite. So, how are you today?" Paul said with a warm smile.

Nancy nervously fidgeted with her skirt. "I'm fine, and I need to get back to class."

"Let's talk for a bit first. How do you like that class? The one you need to get back to?" Paul asked.

Ms. Harman had been making various calls and was on her last one. "Thank you, Mrs. Renolds. We'll be there." Harman hung up the phone. She hurried out of her office and down the hall.

Nancy walked out of Wick's office. When she saw Harman, she turned in the opposite direction, away from Harman, and continued down the hall.

Harman entered Wick's office. Paul was making some notes regarding Nancy.

"If we can postpone Billy's appointment, will you go with me to talk to Katherine's mother? She's at work, but she said she will give us ten minutes," Harman requested.

"Of course, but I want to keep Billy's appointment first. We'll still have time to see Mrs. Renolds before I go to Hudson High," Paul responded.

"Okay," Harman replied harshly and exited.

Paul followed her. "Wait. Don't you want to know what happened with Nancy?"

"Not now," Harman said, and Paul looked surprised. "If she didn't tell you anything, I'll be disappointed. If she did, then I'll be mad that she talked to you instead of me." Harman walked off quickly, looking straight ahead.

Judith stared at her computer and thought pensively. She shook her head. *Paul's right. But this video's finished; it will have to go as it is.* Judith searched for a number and pushed the phone buttons. "Charlie, are there any educational tools planned to deal with family members being the offenders?" Judith scowled impatiently. "I don't care about funding or votes. The children and teens should be the priority."

Chapter Six

Brutal Honesty Is Refreshing

Paul went straight to Billy Langford's office. "You have an appointment for me?"

"Yeah, Terry, seventeen. I think she was molested at thirteen. There was some official involvement, but no charges or prosecutions happened. I don't know the details," Billy said. Paul tapped his leg with two of his fingers and patiently waited.

"Terry seemed okay, but the last few months she's changed a lot. She's acting like a hooker—the way she dresses, her makeup, and her actions." Billy shrugged his shoulders and shook his head. "It's hard to believe she's the same sweet girl who once walked these halls. Something's wrong or has happened. She won't talk to me, and she won't talk to Harman, for sure. Will you give it a shot?"

"As soon as she can come," Paul responded.

"She's waiting in the secretary's office. I knew you'd say yes. I warn you, Doc, she's rather bitter," Billy cautioned. Paul gave a reassuring nod.

Billy smiled. "I'll get her. You can use my office. There's more privacy. No windows. I'm sure glad this program got started," Billy admitted, then left to get Terry.

Paul wanted more details about what happened to Terry at thirteen. He hoped there were some official records.

Billy returned and encouraged Terry to enter. "Terry, come on in."

"Aaaww, Mr. Langford," Terry groaned.

"You promised," Billy reminded her.

Terry entered, chewing a large wad of gum. She stretched and yawned.

"This is Dr. Brandon," Billy said, and motioned toward Paul.

"Hello, Terry," Paul smiled, but did not offer his hand to shake.

"Hey, look, Shrink. I don't want to waste your time, and I don't want you wastin' mine, either," Terry responded sarcastically.

Billy took a deep breath. "Terry, you promised you'd at least hear what he has to say."

"All right! All right! Don't have a coronary." Terry sat down and pulled a long string of gum from her mouth.

"I'll be back." Billy gave Paul a "good luck" look as he closed the door.

Judith and Becky were talking at the reception desk. They were having a friendly chat.

"I'm waiting for Penny's mother. She should be here any minute," Judith said.

Just then, Freda Johnson stepped out of the elevator with a scowl. She was fortyish, average height, but plain, and very thin. She had what is sometimes called waitress black hair from coloring it many shades too dark for her complexion. *Oh, the video Queen has arrived*, Judith thought to herself,

Judith walked toward the elevator. "Freda, I'm glad you could come. Thank you."

Freda Johnson was cold and disinterested. "I had to sign some hospital forms anyway."

"Please, let's go into my office," Judith said, motioning the way.

Freda and Judith entered the office. Freda obviously did not want to be there and grimaced with each step.

"Sit down, please." Judith motioned to the chair.

"I don't have very long," she replied, and reluctantly sat.

"We need to talk about Penny," Judith said, hoping desperately to spark some concern.

Freda was irritated with Judith and huffed. "I've already said whatever the doctors want to do is fine. I've turned her over to the hospital and the state."

"Would you please talk to Penny? I've been told you haven't seen her, and we think it might help. It won't take long." Judith grasped for any humanity in the woman that she could uncover.

"No. She's all yours," Freda replied emotionlessly.

Judith hid her anger. "Are you afraid you'll get upset if you see her?"

"No, lady. I'm heading south for the beach tomorrow, and I've still got shopping to do. Jake's picking me up in twenty minutes." Freda stood up to leave.

Judith was desperate. "Freda, Penny may die!" Judith stated emphatically.

"Then her father can have custody," she sarcastically retorted.

Judith was shocked but forced herself to continue. "Please. Won't you see Penny for just five minutes?"

"No, lady. I'm done."

Freda tried to leave, and Judith grabbed her arm. "How can you go lie in the sun knowing Penny's condition?"

Freda glared at Judith and jerked her arm free. "Don't try that conscience trash with me; it won't work. Go let your bleeding heart drip on somebody else." Freda adamantly walked toward the door, followed by Judith.

"You're right, that conscience trash won't work on you, because you don't have one! I'm pursuing legal charges against you." Judith gritted her teeth and clenched her fist.

Freda stomped out of Judith's office. Judith followed, leaned out of her office door, and yelled as Freda went down the hall. "I hope you get skin cancer from that sun."

Becky was holding the phone, and her mouth dropped.

"I don't believe I said that. But that woman." Judith turned and closed her office door.

Becky said into the phone, "You should have seen Dr. Ramsey. I wish Dr. Brandon had been here."

Michael Webster entered the reception area on his bicycle. "Hello," he said to Becky.

"Gotta go," Becky said and hung up the phone. She walked to Michael. "Get that bike out of here; are you nuts?"

"One: I will get my bike out. Two: No, I'm not nuts. Three: Is Dr. B in?"

"No, not till late this afternoon," Becky said, rather rudely.

Michael waved the large envelope he was holding. "I've got some good interviews here. Would you please give this to Dr. B? Tell him I've talked to everyone I could today. I'm going back later tonight at six."

"What does that mean?" Becky asked.

"Give him the message, and he'll understand. Wait." Michael picked up a pad and a pen from the desk and wrote a note. He then taped the note to the envelope he was holding. "Easy. Just give this to Dr. B," Michael said, handing the envelope to Becky. "Thanks."

Michael smiled and rode slowly down the hall. "I told you I'd take my bike out of here," he called back to Becky over his shoulder.

Paul and Terry were talking rather well. "Miss Perkins will be here tomorrow to get you."

Terry smiled. "Great. That means I get outta nutrition class. I'd agree to acupuncture to get outta there. Ol' lady Hansen's a trip but painful to listen to." Mocking Hansen, Terry stood erect and straightened her pretend lapels.

"Now, girls, tap the cup gently, then take a knife and scrape off the excess like this." Terry gestured as she spun her tale. "Do this over your container so there's no waste. You'll save lots of muss and fuss. Giggle, giggle, snort, snort." Terry laughed. "I guess she's not that bad, but she reminds me of Halloween," Terry said.

"Is she a real witch?" Paul asked.

"Good one. No. She's like your trick-or-treat candy. 'Member how ya'd start eating everything? All the candy you could. Pretty soon ya'd feel sick because of all the sweetness?" Terry described.

Paul nodded his head and smiled.

"Well, she's like that. You can only take so much of her, then ya wanna puke. She's so sweet all the time—it's nauseating."

Paul laughed. "Good one."

"She's only gotten mad once. Beth Kruger found this old book called *The Happy Hooker*, and we were passing it around in class and got caught." Terry put her arms up and wiggled her hands as she rolled her eyes. "Boy, did she go off. She told us to think about what prostitution is, and what would happen if it spread. She even made us write an essay."

"What happened?" Paul asked.

"I did what she said and thought about what would happen if it did spread."

Paul watched intently as Terry gestured.

"So, I put all this stuff in my essay like the airport rent-a-car had a 'Happy Honker' from Hurts. H-U-R-T-S." Terry pointed at Paul. "You couldn't rent it by the week, only for one-night stands." Terry subdued her animated gestures and became serious. "The kicker was that it wouldn't take you anywhere. It only drove in a vicious circle. If you wanted to get somewhere, you had to rent a family car." Terry became quiet.

"Why, Terry, how profound," Paul observed.

"Hansen didn't think it was profound. She thought

it was a Pro found. I believe she really thought I was hooking," Terry said sadly.

The bell rang as Billy knocked and opened the door. "Time to go. You can't be late," he announced.

"Come on in and join the party," Terry said.

"Harman's waiting for you," Billy warned Terry.

"Uuuggh," she groaned.

Terry and Paul joined Billy in the hall. Walking down the corridor faster than the guys, Terry turned back to Paul and Billy, making a silly face. They truly cherished seeing some joy emanating from Terry.

Later, Paul and Billy were talking in the main Guidance Office. Terry energetically ran into the room.

"I survived Harman," she said. "That's another lady who's wired too tight. Whoooa!" Terry rolled her eyes and got excited. "I just realized, it's not their fault. They can't help it. They begin as a joke. It's their names. Harman, Hansen—Ha Ha—get it?"

Billy laughed. Paul rolled his eyes and smiled. "Ohhh," he muttered, then sighed.

"See ya tomorrow," Terry said and waved.

Paul laughed. "Bye, Terry. You're a good kid."

"Shhh. You'll ruin my reputation," Terry said as she stepped out and closed the door.

"Doc, I thought she'd cut you to shreds. What

happened when you talked?" Billy asked.

"She sliced me up pretty well before she decided I wasn't the enemy," Paul admitted.

"Well? How'd it go?" Billy questioned adamantly.

"I'm very concerned about her. Behind that hard, flighty pretense, there's an extremely hurt girl who's on a suicide mission. Something has happened," Paul said.

Billy was shocked. "What?"

Paul nodded. "Terry is so clever, witty, and smart. She has such potential. Has she always been like that?"

"Yes. But her grades have dropped so low that if they don't improve drastically soon, she won't graduate," Billy explained.

Paul looked down. "It's hard to worry about graduating when you can hardly make it through the day."

"Doc, come on. I figured something's bugging her, but she's not that bad. I see her having fun with her friends, laughing and having a good old time," Billy said.

"You've heard the expression, 'die laughing.' Well, in some cases, it's more factual than people realize. The class clown and 'the life of the party' often feel very alone and are just crying out for help." Paul looked seriously at Billy. "You need to look at the whole picture. And when I look at Terry, I see a road map for disaster."

Billy was shocked. He did not know what to say as

he stood silent with his mouth open. Finally, he took a deep breath and said, “Guess that's why you’re the doc. At least I get my summers free.”

“Don't sell yourself short, Billy. Without your insight and understanding, you’d never have suspected a problem. Will you investigate and find out what happened years ago, and get any clues to what's happening now? It would help a lot.”

Billy jumped at the opportunity to help. “Sure. Julie Cramer would probably know.”

“Will she tell Terry you talked to her?” Paul asked.

“Don't worry.” Billy smiled. “Julie owes me. I caught her skipping class and didn't turn her in.”

“Why, Billy, that sounds a bit like blackmail.”

“Oh no, Doc, it's collective bargaining. I collect, then I bargain. Like, there was a guy, Grahm, who was going to drop out of school. Well, some boys, including Grahm, broke into the school, and Grahm dropped his wallet. No damage, just prank stuff. But I found his wallet. The police were here, the whole bit. I never said a word about the wallet.

“The next day, I gave Grahm a choice of graduating with a C average or going to jail. Boy, I scared him good.

“Then I figured, why not go for broke. I acted like I knew who his buddies were and told him that if I got their C-average report cards, I wouldn't rat. That next quarter, I had five report cards on my desk.” Billy chuckled and continued, shaking his head.

"I had no idea who the others were, and the police thought there were only three. But they all graduated, and two even went on to college." Billy beamed.

"I wish there were more counselors like you, Billy. You actually and sincerely care," Paul said joyously.

Chapter Seven

Battling Buried Trauma

Judith and Carl were talking in Judith's office. Carl listened intently.

"You wouldn't have believed that woman. I have never seen anyone so cold and unfeeling! Paul's going to hit the ceiling," Judith said adamantly.

"Frankly, I wish I had seen you place that skin cancer curse on Penny's mother. I've never seen anybody get you that riled," Carl said with a grin.

"If you tell anybody about that, you're in for it."

"What? Do you have a Dr. Denton voodoo doll? Just kidding; your secret's safe with me."

"Good. I hope that's true of Becky, as well," Judith hesitantly admitted.

The phone rang. Carl looked at the time and then chuckled.

"I had no idea psychologists were so insecure," he said.

"That's not insecurity. It's self-preservation." Judith smiled.

Becky rushed into the office. "Dr. Denton, Dr. Denton. They need you on the fourth floor immediately. I was told to get you and tell you it's Penny Johnson, code blue."

Carl and Judith both rushed out of the room and headed to Penny. Becky picked up Judith's phone and pushed three numbers. "Anna, what's a code blue?" She paused. "Somebody's possibly dying?"

Several doctors and nurses were returning items to the crash cart. Carl and Judith rushed into the room. A nurse looked at Carl and Judith, then shook her head. Carl hurried to Penny.

"Penny! Penny!" Carl shouted.

Dr. Scott walked to Carl. "We've done the meds, electric shock, everything. It's no use. Frankly, we've been expecting this."

Carl was angry and upset. He glared at Dr. Scott. "Well, keep trying!" he shouted.

Judith touched Carl's arm. "Calm down, seriously, or

we'll need a crash cart for you."

Carl looked at Penny and spoke harshly. "Penny, Penny Johnson, you come here right now."

"I know how much you care, Carl, but look at her. It's too late," Judith pleaded.

"No! Penny, remember, we're going to the zoo, and we're taking Ben with us. And we're going to the park..." Carl said frantically.

Judith interrupted. "Carl, please."

Carl would not stop. "Penny. Please, please stay with us! Stay for Ben!" Carl cried urgently.

Judith was frightened for Carl's well-being. She had never seen him so upset. Carl was always the one to keep everybody else calm. Judith touched Carl's back.

Tears streamed down Carl's cheeks. "Scooter, please don't go!" Carl pleaded. "Please stay, Scooter! Ben needs you! We all do! Scooter, PLEASE stay!"

There was a long pause, and then BLEEP, BLEEP. Penny's heart started to beat. Carl leaned over the child and gathered her in his arms. As he held her gently, he tried to hide his tears.

Everyone was amazed, especially Dr. Scott. He felt he should listen to Penny's heart and check her vitals. But he didn't want to get that close to Carl. Scott was embarrassed and a little nervous. He whispered to an intern to check out Penny when he had the chance.

A nurse gasped. "Her vital signs are back up on the monitor."

People began to exit the room. Judith touched Carl's shoulder. "Wow," she said.

Carl held Penny for what seemed like an extremely long time. He wiped his eyes with his shirt sleeve and took some deep breaths. Carl gently laid Penny down and straightened his jacket. He looked at the nurse.

"Stay with her; she's not to be left alone ever," Carl instructed.

Carl left the room and entered the hall. People from the code were talking. Many were astonished at what had happened. Carl grabbed Dr. Scott's lab coat and pushed him against the wall.

"Don't you ever—EVER end a code blue that quickly again!" Carl forced himself to calm down and let go of Scott's lab coat. "All of you, in the conference room. NOW."

Everyone headed to the closest conference room. No one said a word as they walked. Carl lingered, not wanting to leave Penny. Judith came out of Penny's room. "Her vital signs look good," she told Carl.

"Can you wait for me?" Carl asked.

"Of course. I'll stay with Penny."

Everyone silently waited for Carl in the conference room. Some exchanged looks, while others were frozen. All remained completely quiet. Carl arrived at the door. His hands were clenched. His jaws were pulsing. Carl paused, entered, and began to address those in the room.

"Dr. Scott. And I use the title loosely. You were the senior person in charge. So, you will get the most heat." Carl slowly and sternly looked around the room. "But you are all guilty." Carl looked at everyone individually again and back at Scott.

"Were you ever a Boy Scout?" Carl asked Scott.

"No, sir," Scott replied.

"Of course not, because in simple first aid you learn that the body can go without oxygen for four to six minutes with no brain damage. Never stop a code before that time has long passed," Carl said adamantly.

Dr. Scott tried desperately to defend his position. "But it had . . .."

Carl interrupted. "Had NOT been sufficient time. I know exactly how long it takes me to respond to a code blue from every corner of this building." Carl showed a key. "I have an elevator override key with me at all times." Carl looked around at everyone. "There is only one area that cannot be reached in time. If I were in the basement and had to get to the top floor."

Carl turned to one of the nurses. "Nurse Carpenter, what's on the top floor of this building?"

Nurse Carpenter was nervous but managed to respond. "Personnel, Payroll, Supply."

"Anyone like to venture a guess as to why there are

no patients there? Get the picture?" Carl said.

Carl gestured to those other than Scott. "Did any of you feel the code was over too soon? The crash cart was already being tidied by the time I arrived."

Nurse Mosley responded. "Yes. I even told Rob I bet they would be doing more if she were a paying customer."

Carl continued. "Next question."

"Sure," Nurse Mosley said confidently.

"Who's worse? Someone who does something wrong but thinks he's right, or someone who knows something's wrong but does nothing to change or stop it?" Carl asked,

"But, sir, he's a doctor," Nurse Mosley protested.

"To answer the question: they're both wrong." Carl looked at Mosley. "And to answer your statement: he's a doctor, and you're a nurse. Both to be considered functioning, capable human beings. And both should be strongly dedicated to helping others."

Mosley lowered her head. Carl resumed.

"Besides, people should stand up for what's right. I don't care if it's the U.S. Surgeon General. If someone's doing something wrong, SPEAK UP! We don't live in the dark ages."

Heads began to lower.

"Give me a conscientious nurse over a careless doctor any day. For that matter, give me a good Boy Scout over both, because he will stand up for what's right every time, without hesitation."

Mosley looked at Carl. "I'm sorry, sir. I think they changed it to just Scouts."

"Whatever. Just making a point. And they must still take the Scout Oath and Law, I certainly hope. Now I know some of the rest of you also thought as Nurse Mosley did." Carl walked around looking at each of them. "Going to a restaurant or a movie you don't like, because you won't speak up, is one thing. But when it comes to the critical issues of life, you must say something!"

Nurse Brown began to cry.

"I promise you, no one will ever be reprimanded for speaking up in this hospital. You'll be applauded." Carl stopped and gave a stern glare. "I can also promise that as long as I'm here, if any of you are involved in another situation like this, you'll immediately be dismissed. Do I make myself clear?"

Carl looked around the room. Heads lowered further as he scanned the group.

"Thank you," Carl concluded. Carl left the conference room and headed to Penny's room.

Nurse Fowler broke the silence. "Who does he think he is? He can't talk to us that way."

Dr Scott replied, "Oh, yes, he can and should. He's ultimately responsible for the life or death of every person in this hospital." Everyone looked at Scott. "What amazes me is, after so many years, so much death, so many patients, he still cares. This isn't just a business to him, it's a stewardship."

Scott turned to Nurse Fowler. "You have a daughter, don't you?"

"Yes," Nurse Fowler responded.

"What if that had been her in Penny's room?" Dr. Scott asked.

Shock and silence filled the room.

Paul and Ms. Harman entered the Trust Savings and Loan Company, where Katherine's mother worked. There was one customer ahead of them.

"She said she could only give us ten minutes?" Paul inquired.

"Yes. I was glad to get that. She's never agreed to see anybody before," Harman replied.

"I am already so late, I let my next school know I'd be delayed or may not even get there today. Did you or the school ever get hold of Katherine?" Paul asked.

"No, the phone's still busy. She's probably talking to Babbs. Oh, I didn't say that you're a doctor. I didn't want to scare her off," Harman admitted.

The customer was escorted to a loan professional and entered the office. The receptionist returned and repeated her standard phrase. "May I help you?"

"I'm Ms. Harman, and this is Mr. Brandon. We have

an appointment to see Mrs. Renolds."

"She's expecting you. It's the large corner office on the right."

They headed to Mrs. Renolds' office. As they walked, Paul said, "'Mr. Brandon.' I haven't heard that in years. So, what's in a title?"

"Well over a hundred thousand more than I make. Or would that be two hundred thousand more?" Harman responded just as they reached the office.

Slightly chubby Mrs. Renolds greeted them immediately. "Come in, come in," she directed.

"Thank you for seeing us. I'm Ms. Harman, and this is Mr. Brandon," she gestured as she spoke.

"Have a seat," Renolds responded. "Now, what can I do for you? I always support the school. Our company name is on the sponsor list every year."

"Yes, you've been quite generous," Harman said. "Well, we want to discuss Katherine with you."

"Has she been giving you trouble?" Renolds asked.

"Oh no. Katherine is a lovely girl. Is she sick today? She hardly ever misses school," Harman inquired.

"She didn't look well, so my husband and I thought she'd better stay home and rest. They always say, 'an ounce of prevention'...however that goes."

Harman forced a smile. "Yes. Well, I . . . ."

Paul gave a concerned look and interrupted. "Are your boys sick?"

"Oh, heavens no. They're as healthy as can be."

Paul looked at his watch. “Oh, our time is up.” Quickly standing, Paul took Harman's arm and led her to the door. Harman and Mrs. Renolds both looked confused, but Paul kept moving.

“We'd like to make another appointment when you have more time,” Paul said.

“It was nice meeting you. Thank you again,” Harman said as they stepped away.

“Nice meeting you too,” Mrs. Renolds called after them.

Paul rushed Harman out of the building. “Come on,” he said.

Harman stopped. “What was that all about? Do you know how long I've waited to meet with her?”

“Look, according to my calculations, there's a good chance Katherine's at home alone with her father,” Paul replied firmly.

“Oh, no! How did I miss that?” Harman lamented.

“Do you know where she lives?” Paul asked.

“No,” Harman answered in a panic.

“Do you have the address?” he asked.

“It's at the school,” she groaned.

“Call the school and get it. The GPS will get us there. We need to get to Katherine ASAP!” Paul stressed.

Chapter Eight

Scum Is Indestructible

Paul and Harman stood on Katherine's front porch. Harman banged on the door and called for Katherine. There was a large half-circle window across the top part of the door, and long, rectangular windows going down each side of the door.

"Katherine. Katherine, it's Ms. Harman from school," she yelled.

Harman and Paul heard Katherine's father close to the door as he spoke harshly. They could see him through the windows lining the front door. He slurred his words, and they could hear his drool gurgling in his throat as he loudly screamed.

"Go away! We ain't buyin' nothin'," Gerald Renolds

shouted, as he stumbled.

Ms. Harman panicked. She turned to Paul. "He's drunk," she said.

"Tell him who you are," Paul quietly instructed.

"Mr. Renolds, this is Ms. Harman from the high school. I must see Katherine immediately."

Gerald hit his fist against the door. "You'll see her when she goes back to school. She ain't truant. Now, GO AWAY," he yelled.

"Mr. Renolds, please open the door. I need to talk to you. I need to see Katherine," Harman called.

"I ain't talkin' to no old maid school buttinski. Now git!" Gerald shrieked.

"Let me talk to Katherine now, Mr. Renolds," Harman said firmly.

"Fat chance," Gerald responded.

Paul motioned to Harman. "Call Katherine again," he encouraged.

"Katherine, can you hear me?" Harman yelled.

Renolds banged the door with his fist again. "No, Katherine can't hear you," he yelled.

Harman looked at Paul. "Maybe she's with Babbs," she said hopefully.

"No, she's here," Paul replied emphatically. Paul raised his voice and forcefully addressed Renolds. "Gerald, this is Dr. Brandon with County Services. We must see Katherine now. Immediately."

A glass crashed against the wall. "You can see her

at school. Now git!" Gerald shouted, and he hit the door with his fist again.

Paul motioned to Harman and mouthed, "Go call the police."

Harman was shocked but said, "Mr. Renolds, I'm going . . .."

Paul stopped Harman. "No. Don't tell him what you're doing."

Harman covered her mistake. "I'm going to talk to Katherine. You might as well open the door," she said.

Another glass crashed against the door. Paul handed Harman the car keys to get her phone and motioned for her to go. Harman rushed to the car parked on the left side of the house.

"Gerald, if you don't want to open the door, please let Katherine talk to us from there," Paul said.

Paul listened and knocked, but he received no response. Paul heard sounds from a room on the right side of the house. It was a girl sobbing. He assumed it was Katherine crying. Paul ran in the direction he heard the weeping. There was an open window that was blocked by a screen. He tried to pull the screen forward.

"Katherine! Katherine!" he shouted. Paul examined the window. He heard her sobs and then saw Katherine huddling into a ball on the floor close to the window. She was a disheveled mess and crying so hard she could barely breathe. "Katherine, can you move far away from the window?"

"Now come on, Katherine," Gerald said, and Paul heard.

"Katherine, I'm coming," Paul yelled.

Paul ran to the front door and tried to break it down. He used his whole body to pound the door multiple times and kicked the lock frantically. Finally, he took a pot from the porch and broke the long, rectangular window lining the door near the lock. Paul put his hand through the broken window and unlocked the door. He quickly entered the house and ran toward the sound of sobbing and gasping. Paul ran to the room on the side.

"What was that?" Gerald asked in surprise.

Paul desperately entered the room. Renolds was dismayed and very drunk. Paul looked at Katherine. She was now huddled in the corner by the window. There was lipstick smeared all over her face. Her clothes were torn, and she was fiercely crying.

Paul moved toward Katherine, and Renolds put his arm out to stop him. Paul looked at Katherine's state and pushed Renolds out of the way, even though Renolds outweighed Paul by a hundred pounds.

"You slime!" Paul said, outraged.

They scuffled. Renolds hit Paul. Paul hit Renolds. They fought briefly, and Renolds fell to the floor unconscious, more from the alcohol than the blows. Paul's head and face were bleeding. Paul walked over to Katherine, removed his coat, and covered her.

"It's all right, Katherine. I'm here with Ms. Harman from school. She'll be inside here soon. Do you know where Babbs is?" Paul attempted to calm Katherine's fears, which were many.

"Dr. Brandon? Katherine?" Harman called as she made her way through the house.

"That's Ms. Harman now. I'm going to get her. She'll be right here," Paul said, trying to be comforting.

Paul hurriedly caught Harman. Harman looked at Paul's face. "What happened to you?" she asked.

"You need to get in there to Katherine. Details later." Paul pointed the way.

Harman started to go, and Paul stopped her. "Wait. You must keep yourself together. Remain calm and assure Katherine that she and everything will be fine," he said, and Harman nodded. "How you react will determine how she handles this," Paul explained.

"Okay," Harman replied and hurried into the room. "Katherine, it's Ms. Harman. It's okay, honey. We're getting you out of here. Everything's going to be okay. I promise."

Harman helped Katherine stand and put Paul's coat on her completely. "I'm taking you to the car. Dr. Brandon will gather some of your things," she told her.

Katherine was rigid and scared. However, she was thankful Ms. Harman was there. She did not say one word.

Paul looked at Katherine. "Ms. Harman is taking you

to see Babbs right now. You will be with Babbs very soon," he assured Katherine.

Harman looked at Renolds on the floor and then at Paul. Harman and Katherine left immediately. Paul looked around Katherine's room and found a large shopping bag. He gathered some clothes, a hairbrush, two pairs of shoes, a jacket, and a toothbrush. Renolds did not move.

"That poor kid. This is criminal. But will your drunken face go to jail? No, you disgusting piece of sludge. It's guys like you that give males a bad name. You self-indulgent pervert," Paul vented as he gathered the items.

Harman returned. "Katherine wants her teddy bear that's hidden under the bed to keep him safe." She looked at Renolds. "Is he dead?"

"To quote him, 'Fat chance,'" Paul growled. "Haven't you heard, 'Only the good die young?'"

"What happened? How'd you get in here?" Harman asked.

"I think it's commonly called 'breaking-and-entering.' But I had no choice."

"You had a choice; you just made the right one," Harman smiled.

Paul picked up a glass of water from the nightstand and threw the water in Gerald's face. Renolds stirred and moaned.

"See, scum is indestructible," Paul smirked.

They heard the siren of a police car getting closer. "I see you made the phone call," Paul said.

Harman panicked. "Katherine," she said, and ran toward the front door.

"I'll bring her stuff. And the bear," Paul called after her.

Harman quickly walked down the driveway. Two policemen walked from their patrol car.

"We're looking for a Ms. Harman," Officer Gilcrest said.

"I'm Ms. Harman. I phoned you."

"You work at the high school, right?" he asked.

"Yes," she answered.

Paul exited the house with Katherine's things and walked to Harman. Gilcrest looked at Katherine in the car.

"What seems to be the trouble?" Gilcrest inquired.

Paul handed Harman Katherine's belongings and her teddy bear. Whispering, Paul told Harman, "She needs to get with Babbs, and you'll need to prepare Babbs. Her reaction will play a huge part in Katherine's recovery."

Harman addressed the police officers. "This is Dr. Brandon from County Services."

Paul extended his arm, and they shook hands. "I'm Officer Gilcrest. This is O'Reilly."

"Can we step inside?" Paul asked. "These two ladies need to leave." Paul motioned for Harman to go.

Officer O'Reilly pointed to Katherine. "Looks like she needs to be examined." Then he motioned to Harman and said, "And she needs to make a statement."

"They will be happy to meet us at the precinct. They need to attend to a few things, like getting the young lady's sister."

Paul motioned again for Harman to leave. "We'll meet you at the police station," Paul called.

"We'll be there," Harman replied. Harman rushed into the car and left with Katherine to find Babbs immediately. She did not want them to get detained.

Officer Gilcrest said, "Well, you are the doc. And you're with County Services, so that should be okay."

"Please, officers, let's go inside. Thank you for responding so quickly," Paul said, leading the way to the house.

"We were in the area," Officer O'Reilly added.

The police car was in the street in front of the house. Gerald staggered to the front door and shouted his slurred words while he pointed at Paul.

"Ofsifer, arresth that man," Gerald screamed. "And that woman who was here too!"

Harman had already driven away quickly to spare Katherine any more trauma.

Becky was at her reception desk. She had a mirror

on the desk, squeezing a small bump on her forehead. Loni Hillerman entered the area, and Becky grabbed a tissue.

“Oh, hi,” Becky greeted her.

“Hi, Becky. I need to know where Dr. Brandon is right now.”

I can't tell you,” Becky said firmly.

“You have to,” Loni insisted.

“Sorry, but he said anybody other than O’Connor or Benson will have to wait,” Becky explained.

“Well done, Becky. I know you are trying to be conscientious, but I must get this envelope to him,” Loni said.

Becky blankly stared at Loni. Loni held up the package.

“Look, he needs this immediately. Paul called this morning and asked me to get some information on this man I know. It's extremely important!” Loni said.

“You're right when you said I'm being conscientious, but Dr. Brandon thinks I'm a ditz. I must prove that I'm good,” Becky confessed.

“I'm sure Dr. Brandon doesn't think you're a ditz, and he would want you to help me. And help him,” Loni encouraged.

“No way. I have my instructions.” Becky stood firm.

“I know, ‘O'Connor and Benson.’ I heard. Is Dr. Ramsey in?” Loni asked.

“No, and I don't know when she's coming back either.

She told me to handle things."

"Will you call Dr. Brandon at whatever school he's helping? His phone goes straight to voicemail," Loni sighed in frustration.

"No. You're not O'Connor or Benson."

Loni had reached the point of fighting her anger. "This can't wait," she barked.

"It'll have to," Becky insisted.

Loni got huffy as she contemplated her departure. "Please tell Dr. Brandon I was here. And that it is urgent he telephone me." Loni was adamant and left.

Michael entered with his bike again.

"Haven't you ever heard of walking?" Becky snapped.

"Sure, but then I would have to find a bike rack. That's a pain and wastes time," Michael told her.

"So is talking to nut cases. What do you want?" Becky asked.

"I gave you the wrong envelope, and I need my chemistry report," he confessed.

Becky looked for the envelope and then gave it to Michael. He transferred the note he had written and then handed Becky the correct envelope. "Thanks. Now we're good," Michael said.

"So, travel on your way," Becky replied.

Judith and Carl entered the reception area and walked toward Judith's office.

"Are you quite sure you're okay?" Judith asked quietly.

"Yes. I'm fine," Carl insisted.

"You know, I was impressed. Excellent job, Carl. I honestly thought Penny was gone for good."

Judith and Carl entered Judith's office. Michael and his bike left, as the telephone rang. "Drs. Ramsey and Brandon," Becky answered.

It was Loni calling and disguising her voice. "This is Mrs. O'Connor. I need to speak with Dr. Brandon, please."

"Oh yes, Mrs. O'Connor. He'll return your call very shortly. Where can he reach you?" Becky jotted down the telephone number Loni provided. The other telephone line rang. "He'll get right back to you, Mrs. O'Connor. Goodbye," she said.

Becky answered the call. It was Paul. "I was just about to call you. Mrs. O'Connor called, and she wants to talk to you right now!"

Paul quickly wrote the number Becky gave him for Mrs. O'Connor on his hand. That was his only option at the time.

Paul entered the police station. "Sergeant, is there an office I can use? I need to call a patient."

The sergeant motioned with his head toward the left. "In there," he said.

Paul immediately headed to the designated room,

as the sergeant laughed. "You might want to call your lawyer while you're at it."

Taking a deep breath, Paul called the number Becky had given him, and Loni answered. "Paul, it's Loni. Using O'Connor was the only way I could get you."

Paul laughed. "Smart move."

"Thanks. I called that creep I said I'd never speak to again. You've got to be at his place no later than six thirty. He's leaving town. I got his demo samples. I'll bring them to you."

"Thanks. I really appreciate it," Paul replied.

"Anytime. It's Buzzy Kaden. K B Casting. He often uses just the initials and talks fast, so people think he's from a big network." Loni imitates Buzzy. "'I'm from K.B.C.' You'll see what I mean. He's so slick, I think he showers in Vaseline. It's 149 Glen Eagles Drive, Suite 306. Good luck," she said. Loni hung up laughing. "Vaseline," she chuckled. "Pretty good."

Judith and Carl were in her office. They had discussed all the current problems and planned some new strategies.

"I'll call you after my next patient is gone," Judith promised. "She should be here shortly. This is the case you have that new intern working on. The bright, well-mannered one. What's his name?" she asked.

"You must mean Preston McCall," Carl remembered.

"Yeah. He's super nice." Judith smiled.

"How's he doing?" Carl inquired.

"Fine. But we gave him a genuinely tough case to follow. Hillary Fletcher is beautiful, intelligent, and financially secure. She has four wonderful children and a lovely home."

Carl ventured a guess. "Her husband's abusive?"

"Nope. Her husband is extremely handsome and completely devoted to his family."

Carl scratches his chin. "What gives?" he asked.

"Well, after work, he helps her with dinner, homework, dishes, everything. When the children are in bed, he usually fixes Hillary's favorite milkshake and gives her a back rub," Judith described.

"So, what's the problem? They have a rotten sex life?" Carl guessed.

"No, they have a great sex life. That comes after the milkshake and back rub."

Carl raised his eyebrows and put up his hands. "So, what is it?" he asked in frustration.

"On the surface, she says the problem is that her husband is boring. Try dropping that one on a new intern." Judith sighed.

"Let me guess. One last chance." Carl decided she was average case number fifteen, bored with her life, and having an identity crisis.

Judith shook her head no. "We've gone through all

of that. Boy, is this kid getting some rough on-the-job training. Hillary met this man . . .."

Carl interrupted, "She was determined to have an affair," he said excitedly, thinking he had gotten the answer.

Judith looked Carl directly in the eyes. "Affairs, Carl. This is not your typical have one relationship, eventually run home, glad you didn't get caught."

Carl scratched his cheek. He was baffled.

"Hillary is having multiple affairs where each guy thinks he's the only love of her life. Frankly, I don't know how she pulls it off."

Judith shook her head and put her hand on her face.

"You're kidding? You're putting me on? Right?" Carl asked.

"NO. She knows if she gets caught, she could lose everything. I'm afraid, subconsciously, that's what she's after. She even says her husband should have full custody of the children."

Judith knocked over her pen holder as she gestured, but she caught it. "Hillary justifies all this game playing because she's afraid of catching some disease. Otherwise, she says, she'd have one-night stands."

"She could still get a disease," Carl responded.

"Yes, but she's certainly lessened the odds," Judith said with one eyebrow raised. "The only one her victims have sex with is her."

Carl was shocked. "Victims! How many men are we

talking about? Three? Four?"

"Presently, try eleven. It may be twelve by today," Judith shrugged her shoulders and gave a questioning look. "Again, I don't know how she does it!"

"Wait a minute," Carl objected. "You're telling me this lady has eleven men, plus her husband, all being faithful to her. I don't believe it. She's got to be fantasizing these guys."

"No. They are real. Preston even followed her to three of her rendezvous, because he couldn't believe it either. I'll never forget that day he came into my office."

Judith described the conversation she had with Preston. "Carl, he was livid. 'Dr. Ramsey, I'm not handling this situation very well. This woman makes me ill. I want to punch her, and I don't even believe in guys hitting females.'

"What happened? I asked. Preston looked at me like he was expecting chastisement. But, of course, I gave him none, and he continued.

"'Well, I couldn't believe all these men were real, so I followed her. There she went, one after another, falling all over herself every time. She was so convincing; if I hadn't known better, I would have sworn she was in love with each of them.'

"I have to admit, Carl, I was a bit shocked," Judith said. "Then Preston added more.

"'And between men, she went to lunch with her husband. What a nice guy. I just wanted to tell the poor sap everything. Patient confidentiality stinks.'

"Well-mannered Preston even hit his fist on the desk. 'How can we help Hillary?' I asked him. 'What do you think is truly bothering her?' And he went off.

"'Bothering her? Not a thing! That lady. Lady? Woman...person doesn't have a conscience. Nothing's bothering her. As for help, how about helping the poor snooks she's taken in?' Preston was angry but continued.

"'After she left, I went up to the last guy and told him his wife was pretty. Then this idiot told me she wasn't his wife yet, but he is praying someday she will be!'

"Preston put his hands up in disgust and persisted. 'This jerk's praying for her to be his wife. Finally, I understand what my mom meant when she told me to be careful what I pray for because I just might get it.

"'I'm telling you, if Freud had met Hillary Fletcher, there would be no psychiatry today, only capital punishment for adultery.'

"Preston was a wreck. By this time, he was moving all around the room. I had to tell him to have a seat. I was concerned he was going to have a stroke or something. He immediately sat down.

"I explained that no matter how Hillary looked or acted on the outside, she was suffering tremendously on the inside. She is still a victim of the sexual abuse she endured as a child. I could tell Preston tried hard not to roll his eyes.

"I told him that with Hillary's father repeatedly molesting her, Hillary bought the myth that all men are rotten. So not only is she out to prove that, but she is also getting back at a few along the way. Preston was still disgusted and talked about all the people Hillary had hurt.

"I agreed and made it clear that being hurt is absolutely no excuse to hurt others. I told him that Hillary has no real self-esteem or sense of value. When her mother found out about the molestation, she did nothing to stop it. That destroyed Hillary inside more than Preston could fathom. I explained that she was coming from a bad place. Truly, a horrible place.

"I told him that Hillary doesn't feel worthy of the nice life and family she has now. She is out to destroy it. And I sincerely hope we can turn her around before she does."

Judith paused and looked at Carl. "I just hope this mess doesn't turn Preston against marriage. He's come a long way but still has a good bit to go."

Carl smiled. "He has been through some garbage, for sure, with his parents' divorce. But with you on his side, I'm sure he will be fine."

Judith's intercom buzzed. "Yes?" she answered.

"Hillary Fletcher's here," Becky responded.

"Thank you, Becky. I'll be right out." Judith released the button.

Carl shook his head. "It's so tragic how these sexual

abuse victims lose not only their childhood but much of their adult lives as well," he said.

Judith walked Carl to the door. "I know. The horror certainly doesn't end just because someone turns eighteen or twenty-one. Like other things, you take it with you."

"If I'm not in my office, I'll be in Penny's room," Carl said and stepped out of Judith's office.

"See you later," Judith said.

Carl paused. "Please tell Paul I've arranged for Chinese dinner delivery for three."

"My favorite. Thanks."

Carl smiled and left.

Chapter Nine

Reluctant Soulful Sharing

Judith motioned as she spoke. "Hillary, please come in."

Hillary was bright and attractive. She entered the office, and Judith closed the door.

"Are you feeling all right? You don't look so well," Judith asked.

Hillary threw her purse on a chair and sat down. She gestured with her hands as she talked.

"I'm just tired. I have an appointment tomorrow for a check-up. Well, it finally happened. I got caught."

"What? Tell me about it," Judith encouraged.

"I had decided twelve was my limit. It just takes too much time. My even dozen was Barney White, one of Evan's business partners. He's super cute." Hillary put her head back and placed her hands on her face. "Here we are, after hours, in the locked executive room, naked on the conference table, and in walked Evan with his key."

Hillary looked at the floor. "He had come back to the office for some documents he had forgotten and noticed the lights were on. It must have been a horrific sight."

"How did Evan take it?" Judith asked.

"Oh, he's blaming himself and trying to find out how he failed me. He wants me to forgive him and let him make it up to me." Hillary became cold and sarcastic. "Now, of course, he thinks I'm in love with Barney. Barney thinks I'm in love with Barney. He wants to marry me."

Hillary looked at Judith. "Can you imagine? You don't leave a man named Evan Fletcher for a Barney White."

Judith placed her hands on her desk and looked sternly at Hillary. Hillary did not even look at Judith.

Hillary continued, "If I was going to get caught, why couldn't it have been with Reed Briarton, Stanley Marlow . . .."

"Hillary, come on. This is me you're talking to. I know the pain and anguish that you're carrying inside." Judith walked over and gently took Hillary's hands. "And I think it's way past time you share some of that pain and anguish with your husband. Before it destroys both of you and the children."

Judith and Carl were looking at the food cartons on the desk.

"It's almost eight thirty. Paul said he'd be late, but this is way late. Let's eat. I'm starved," Judith suggested.

"Good idea." Carl pointed to the containers. "There's sweet and sour pork . . .."

Paul knocked and entered. He quickly took off his coat and tossed it on the closest chair. "Sorry I'm so late."

"We were about to give up on you. Where've you been?" Judith asked.

"Everything always takes longer than we plan," Paul said. "At least for me. How's Penny?"

Carl and Judith looked at each other. "Alive, thanks to Carl," Judith said.

"WHAT?" Paul was stunned.

"I'll fix the plates while you fill him in," Judith told Carl.

Two plates were full, and one was empty. "Hey, look fellows, I'm done. You need to eat. You can eat and talk, you know." Judith laughed.

"I like a woman with a healthy appetite," Carl said.

Judith hit Carl with her napkin. “Don't get smart,” she said with a grin.

“I'm not. I'm serious. I can't stand to go out to dinner with people who only order shrimp cocktail or a salad,” Carl confessed.

Paul chimed in. “I know what you mean. Food is one of the pleasures of life that should be enjoyed.”

“Absolutely, Paul,” Carl agreed. “I dated this French girl from Louisiana. When we went out to eat, she ate. None of this ‘eating like a bird’ nonsense. I fell madly in love with her.”

“Does Glenda know about this?” Judith asked.

“It was Glenda. Glenda Bonnet.”

“Carl, you're exactly right. Ask any American bachelor. If you’re not passionate about food, passion for life and in other areas is often lacking, as well.”

Carl picked up his glass, and Paul followed.

“A toast to the Glendas and the Judiths of this world. Real and passionate people.” They took a drink.

“I think you're both exhausted,” Judith observed. “You've been working too hard.”

Carl's intercom buzzed, and he answered it. “Dr. Denton.”

“There's a Buzzy Kaden on line two for Dr. Brandon,” the nurse said.

“I'll take it,” Paul replied.

“Buzzy Kaden?” Judith questioned.

“He’ll take it,” Carl answered. Carl handed Paul the

phone receiver and pushed the button for line two.

"Buzzy, hello. Any luck?" Paul paused to listen. After a moment, he said, "Triple time is fine. I'll be there as quickly as I can." He hung up the phone. "I've got to leave, but I'll be back."

"Who is that guy?" Judith answered.

Paul took a large book off the top of the bookshelf. "I'll explain Buzzy later. But there's something we need to discuss right now. I'm convinced that talking to Penny about playing dolls, Mickey Mouse, and Sesame Street will not work."

"What do you mean?" Judith asked.

"She's been through a horrendous nightmare, and she's got to deal with it."

Carl looked confused. Paul continued, "If a kid gets hurt, we give him or her a cookie or a toy to make it better. But this is too deep with Penny. It can't be covered up or solved with 'make it betters.'"

"But you can't talk to her about what happened yet! Bringing all that up may push her so deep, trying to avoid it, we'd never get her back," Judith insisted.

"Exactly. So, what do we do?" Paul asked.

Judith and Carl both looked puzzled. Paul held up the book. "Fairytales. I've been reading Penny fairytales," Paul explained. Carl and Judith looked at each other, bewildered. Paul continued, "Then I realized it would be much more effective with you two reading them to her. Carl's voice comforts her, and you're a female."

"So, what's the difference between Big Bird and fairytales?" Carl asked. "I get it. You believe Mr. Snuffleupagus is real."

Paul smiled. "What do all traditional fairytales have in common? Something that newer stories don't, to the same degree."

"I'll bite," Carl said. "What is the difference between them?"

"Most fairytales have something horribly rotten going on, but it eventually always works out at the end."

Judith understood immediately. "Aaaawwww."

Paul continued, "Think about it. Hansel and Gretel and the witch's oven. Red Riding Hood's grandmother and the wolf."

"But they all have a happy ending," Judith acknowledged. "And that's what Penny needs to realize. Awful things can happen, but everything can get better. That's brilliant, Paul."

"We'll try it," Carl said excitedly, hoping for anything to help.

Paul grabbed his coat. "Thanks. Did you find out anything about pressing charges against Penny's mother?"

"It's not going so well. The law seems to treat children like property! The parents have the rights, not the kids. Depending on the state, children have no rights at all. You want to toss your kids away like an old pair of shoes, you can. It's a disgrace. But I'm still working on it. Truthfully, I'm on my third lawyer. I'm hoping to find one who actually cares. Right now, the knowledge and hope of accountability in the afterlife is the only thing sustaining me," Judith confessed. "I hope Penny's mom goes to the hottest part of Hades."

"I still can't believe she won't talk to Penny," Paul said.

"I can!" Judith adamantly declared. "She's awful!" Judith took a deep breath and forced herself to calm down. "Paul, don't come back here. Go home and get some rest. You were up all night, and you look awful."

Paul laughed. "Thanks. Bye," he said, grabbing some food to eat on the way as he hurried to his car.

Becky was at her desk when Judith entered the next day.

"Good morning," Judith greeted her cheerfully.

"Good morning. Dr. Brandon asked me to tell you that he's at Hudson High." Becky leaned closer. "I also had to cancel his Friday morning appointments. I overheard that he must go to some hearing thing about a girl named Katherine."

Judith gave Becky a harsh look. She was glad to have the information. However, she did not like Becky eavesdropping. "I'll be in my office for a bit, then I'm going to be with Dr. Denton."

“Well, you told me to schedule that woman. She's coming. I'm afraid it's too late to reach her,” Becky said.

“Which woman?”

“The one who didn't want to see Dr. Brandon; she wanted a woman doctor.”

“I thought I said... never mind. That's fine. What's her name?” Judith asked.

“Marcy Klein,” Becky replied.

Judith walked to her office. “Let me know when she arrives.” Judith put her things down and called Carl.

“Good morning,” Carl said. “How did you sleep?”

Judith laughed. “All night I was chased by wolves and witches. I had forgotten that fairytales were so graphic. I'll be up when I can. See you soon.” She hung up.

Judith's intercom buzzed. “Yes,” Judith answered.

“Mrs. Klein is here,” Becky informed her.

“Please send her in.” Judith opened her door and welcomed her new patient. “Hello, Mrs. Klein. Please come in. I'm Dr. Ramsey.”

They shook hands. Klein limped into the office. “Nice to meet you. I was glad to get to see you so quickly.”

“Please, Marcy, have a seat,” Judith directed.

“Don't call me Marcy!” she snapped. Mrs. Klein composed herself. “I go by M.J.,” she stated emphatically.

“Please, M.J., sit down,” Judith said soothingly.

“Thank you,” M.J. replied and took a seat.

“How can I help you?” Judith purposely asked calmly.

"I'm having a problem with my marital situation. Basically, I think I hate men." Klein struggled to find her words. "Not that I hate all men. There are some that I like; I've learned to like them. But that's rare."

"You said you were having trouble with your marriage. Do you like your husband?" Judith probed.

"Oh yes. He is one of the best. But I don't like for him to touch me. We have no physical relationship whatsoever," she confessed as Judith patiently listened without comment or expression. "I told him he could have an affair or hire a prostitute. He won't. He says he loves me, and he'll wait till we work it out." Klein crossed her arms. "I don't want to work it out. I want to be left alone!"

"Why did you marry him?" Judith inquired.

"You may think I'm terrible, and I was just using him. But I need to be married for political reasons." Klein stood up and paced. "I want to go into politics. For the most part, you get farther if you're married." She sat back down. "Also, I don't want people thinking I am gay or trans. I'm not. I just HATE men, and sex too, I guess."

"Do you have any idea why you feel that way?" Judith asked.

"Oh, I know exactly why I feel like this. It's no deep, hidden secret from my past. It's my entire childhood. Year after rotten year." Klein stared at Judith. "All of this is confidential, right?"

"Of course," Judith reassured her.

"You can't be too careful when it comes to politics." Klein squeezed her hands together tightly. "I'll explain things. Then you can tell my husband to leave me alone and keep my marriage together."

"Case solved, huh? You were telling me about your childhood," Judith encouraged.

"'Childhood.' That has such a nice ring to it. Let's call this my growing up." Klein rubbed her right arm with her left hand. "My father was a sadistic swine. Every night, he slapped my mother around and then had sex with her." Klein looked disgusted. "All over the house. Everywhere. It was fine with her because she never did anything to stop it. They both make me sick!" She paused.

"I'm sorry for being snippy when you called me Marcy. My father, well, my biological sperm donor's name is Marc—spelled with a C. I don't like being named after him, so I go by M.J."

Klein had trouble breathing. "He raped all four of my sisters. Time and time again, and my mother knew it."

"You say he raped your sisters; did he rape you?" Judith prodded.

"He tried, but I was lucky. I was a fast runner. I always got away." Klein motioned to her foot. "You may have noticed I have a slight limp. I can thank him for that. My mother too." Klein made a fist. "As a matter of fact, that's why I went into law. I plan to sue both my parents for what they put me through."

"So, what happened to your foot?" Judith asked sympathetically.

"He decided to rape me one night. I ran outside barefoot. It was freezing; I can still feel the stinging. My teeth even hurt." Klein gritted her teeth and touched her cheeks. "I hid for hours. Until he drank enough to pass out. Anyway, my feet got frostbitten, and part of one had to be removed. Thus, the limp!"

Klein inhaled deeply and continued, "I can still remember seeing my mother while I was lying in the hospital bed of the emergency room. I was barely a teenager. You'll never guess what my mother did. They deserve each other. The doctors were deciding what to do about my foot. My mother leaned down and whispered to me. 'If you tell them how this happened, I'll tell them you're lying, and they'll never believe you. You'll get locked up.' Nice, eh? My own mother. I didn't want to get locked up. Home was bad enough. The five of us . . .."

For the first time, Klein showed sadness. She had been hiding her pain with anger. Klein began again.

"You know, when I told you I was the only one never raped … I said I was a fast runner and lucky. There was more to it than that." Klein became overwhelmed with emotion. She could not speak. Judith sat quietly and waited. She knew it was better for Klein to feel the pain and sadness than to foster the anger and hostility, hiding her wounds and trauma. Klein cried a flood of tears and struggled to breathe.

Slowly, Klein took deep breaths and regained some control. "My sister Ruth. Every time he'd be after me, she'd start yelling at him to leave me alone, and he'd rape her instead!" Klein sobbed.

Judith picked up the box of tissues and offered them to Klein. "Oh, I'm sorry," Klein said and tried to stop crying.

"No, don't be sorry, and don't stop. Just cry. It's good to let it out. Holding it in is what causes many problems. Ruth must love you very much. What a wonderful sister." Judith touched Klein's shoulder. "You were right when you said you were lucky. You're lucky to have a sister like that."

Klein screamed. "To have had. To – have – had! She's dead. Ruth's dead!" Klein was hysterical. "She hemorrhaged to death trying to give herself an abortion. She said she'd rather die than have his baby, and she did."

Judith was completely heartbroken by this tragic tale. However, she kept thinking of what Confucius said about "If you seek revenge, you should dig two graves." She desperately hoped she could help M.J.

Chapter Ten

Some Teens Are Smarter Than They Realize

Paul was at Hudson High. He had an appointment scheduled with Gail. They had met the previous week, and Paul was anxious to continue their discussion.

"Gail, last week you promised you'd tell me the whole story this week, and this week is here," Paul said with his comforting smile.

Gail tried to respond and finally admitted, "I know, but it's so hard."

Paul looked at her with understanding. "Seriously, if you'd be more comfortable talking to someone else, I work with a terrific lady. I know you'd like her."

"No. I don't want to talk to anyone else. I've thought

about it a lot. When you spoke to our gym class, you were so right about what you said. You understand. You get it," Gail explained her reasoning and willingness to try to talk with Paul.

"Thank you, Gail. Please, continue."

Gail was having difficulty getting started. Paul came to her rescue. "I understand that, for years, your mother has often gone to various places, leaving you with your great aunt and uncle."

Gail struggled, and Paul spoke again. "You were telling me about being at a retro old-fashioned drive-in theater to watch a movie. Your great aunt and uncle were in the front seat of the car, and you were asleep in the back. . .."

Suddenly, a woman burst into the room and interrupted Paul. "Dr. Brandon, please come quickly. Please!" Paul recognized the lady as one of the school counselors.

"This is not a good time for me to leave right now," Paul said adamantly.

"It's urgent! A matter of life and death. PLEASE," she said and began to cry.

Paul looked at Gail. "I'm so sorry. I'll be back as soon as I can."

They exited and entered the hallway. Paul asked the counselor, "What is it? What's happening?"

"You've got to talk to Vance Patterson. They've called the police to take him away. You can't let them. He's a great kid, but he's got a gun!" She was petrified. "He's in the Guidance Office. I'll stay with Gail. Please help him."

"Get Gail back in class. She doesn't need any more distress," Paul instructed and went directly to Vance.

Paul tried to get Vance to talk in the Guidance Office. However, it was not working because there were three other adults with them. The three were scared and acted like hostages, which did not help the situation. Paul talked Vance into entering an empty room that was not surrounded by glass. Paul was concerned about what would happen when the police got there. He instructed the three people to leave immediately and to tell the police, when they arrived, that he had the situation totally under control.

Once everyone was gone, Paul locked the Guidance Office door. Then he entered the Vice Principal's office, where Vance waited. Vance was fifteen, slouched over, and sat on the large desk. He held the gun in his right hand and stared at the floor.

Paul chose his words and his actions carefully. "Vance, you said you'd tell me the whole thing privately. I want to help you. Please level with me."

Vance looked at Paul and then back at the floor. Paul continued. "Why did you beat up your history teacher?"

After a long thirty-second pause, Vance replied. "I just couldn't help myself. I hate him so much!"

"That kind of hate doesn't come without a reason," Paul said.

Vance was silent, then started to talk. "I don't know how this all happened. I don't know how I got into such a mess. He seemed like such a nice guy. He was my favorite teacher. We talked about cars and sports; it was great." Vance ran his left hand through his hair. "Then he showed me some bodybuilder magazines and invited me to his house to lift weights. We got together every Tuesday and Thursday night. Schuller would show me racing DVDs and workout videos. It was terrific, like we were best buds."

Vance became quiet and motionless. "Then one night, he showed me some films he had. I'd never seen anything like that. Men and women together. He said he couldn't make it on a teacher's salary." Vance's voice quivered. "He has a small production company where he makes films. He said I'd be great at it and could pick up some easy cash." Vance stopped and was an emotional mess.

"So, you made some films you're afraid someone might see?" Paul said.

"It's worse than that. He said he'd fix me up so no one would recognize me. I don't think you could tell unless they knew it was me." Vance stood up and began to pace. He shook his head. "At first, it was kind of exciting. I talked to two girls I know. They wanted the money and to feel like actresses. See, he wanted me to get girls for the films." Vance started waving the gun around as he paced.

"Take some deep breaths and calm down. You're doing fine. Let's put the gun on the table," Paul gently suggested.

"No," Vance snapped. After a couple of tense moments, Vance calmed himself and lowered the gun. He sat back on the desk. "But when we got to Schuller's, and I tried to follow his instructions, it got tough. It bothered me more than the girls, but he laughed and talked us through it."

Vance looked at Paul like a beaten puppy. "The next day, he had this woman give me lessons. He called them acting lessons. At first, it was exciting. But then it got sickening. I wanted to throw up."

"So, making the films bothered you. And you didn't like what Schuller was making you do," Paul outlined.

"That's true, but that's not what's eating at me. After those two girls made a film, Schuller told me he wanted girls who didn't look so experienced. He wanted younger girls. The first two girls were older than me. So, I thought he wanted girls my age so we would look better together."

Vance looked at the floor once again. He paused for several minutes. Paul gave him time to adjust to what he had already confessed. He began to talk again. "So,

I met a girl at the skating rink who was fourteen, and we made a film."

Paul listened intently. He allowed Vance to stop or pause as often as he needed.

"I went back to the skating rink. Schu wanted girls even younger than Missy. I talked a thirteen-year-old into going, cause that's what Schu wanted. It's like I had to follow his rules and instructions, or I would get in trouble."

With the gun still in his right hand, Vance ran his left hand through his hair. "He said to get someone who hadn't finished reaching puberty. I thought that was strange. I even told him I didn't want to do that. He said I'd better, or my mom would see my films!"

They sat for what seemed an eternity. Finally, Paul said, "That had to be very scary. It's okay. Go on."

"I ended up getting this eleven-year-old little kid to come and make a film. Then there was another eleven-year-old. He kept threatening to show the films to my mom." Vance paced again. "He kept saying, 'One more. Just one more.' Then he wanted me to try for eight- or nine-year-olds. He's sick!"

Vance began sweating profusely. He wiped his forehead with his arm. "I took this little eight-year-old up there." Vance froze and looked at Paul. He said forcefully, "I don't know why these little kids are alone. Somebody should be watching 'em." Vance wiped his nose with his sleeve. "I kept hoping the mothers would come or somebody. But nooo, they just dropped the kids off at the skating rink. Alone. Unattended. Well, the eight-year-old's big sister was there, but she didn't pay any attention to her or where she was."

Paul shook his head in amazement at how irresponsible and stupid adults can be. He thought he would never do that if he were ever blessed enough to have children.

Vance admitted, "I started to lie and say the mothers were there. So I couldn't get anyone. But then I was afraid Schu was having me watched or followed. I never want my mom to see what I've done.

"Anyway, I took this eight-year-old to Schu's, and I thought she was going to fall apart. But, like usual, Schu talked her through it." Vance rubbed his cheek with the gun. "He talks you through it while you're there, but later you feel like garbage! Schu had to make the film with her; I couldn't do it. It made me sick. Schu makes me sick."

Vance was extremely distraught. He rubbed the gun barrel on his throat. "You know, Schu is truly the one who's scum and dirt! But I'm scum and dirt now too, 'cause I helped him!"

"Put the gun down. Please. We don't want any accidents," Paul said.

Vance continued, "I decided I wasn't going to do it anymore. I tried to stop. But what made my mind up was seeing Missy, one of the first girls I got from the skating rink to take to Schu."

Paul said firmly, "Lower the gun and tell me what happened." Vance paused and looked at Paul. He closed his eyes, lowered the gun, and began again.

"Missy looked bad. I mean real bad. I could hardly recognize her. She still hadn't told anyone what had happened. Schu's good at making you feel guilty. Like it's all your fault. So, you won't say anything or tell anybody about what went on."

Tears filled Vance's eyes, and he stared at Paul. "What scares me the most is, if the fourteen-year-old looks so bad, how are the littler ones doing?" Vance cried a flood of remorseful tears.

"Vance, you are right. This guy must be stopped. I'm going to need your help to do that. Please, put the gun down. We can help these girls."

Vance pushed the gun into his neck. "I can't take this pain anymore."

"Wait," Paul reacted quickly. "I need your help, Vance. I need you here to stop Schuller. Don't let him get away with this. I promise the pain will get better. I can't help these kids without you. You need to stay here and help all these kids get better. Together, we've got to stop Schuller. I cannot do it without you. Don't let Schuller win. Think of the girls."

Vance hesitated and thought for several minutes, which felt like hours to Paul. "Vance, I need your help to stop Schu. I cannot do it without you," Paul said.

Vance paused and finally lowered the gun. Paul took it. Paul placed his hand on Vance's shoulder and sighed. “You can get through this. We will stop Schu and help all the girls, and you. You are a victim of Schuller, too. We can do this together.”

Vance cried even harder. “I’m so sorry about the girls. But I'm not sorry I beat up Schu. I just wish I'd killed him!”

Paul rubbed Vance’s shoulder as he cried. “You did the right thing. Death is too good for Schuller. He needs to suffer for a long time—the way he’s made you and the girls suffer. Only harder. Most prison inmates don’t take too kindly to anyone who has hurt children. With all the films he’s made, it should be easy to get him put in jail—where he belongs. We can do this. You can save these girls from a lifetime of misery and nightmares. And probably many other kids too.”

Chapter Eleven

Adults Can Be Clueless and Cruel

Carl was talking to two nurses at the nurses' station. He was tremendously upset.

"Attempted suicide? How old is she?" Carl asked.

Maria, the shorter nurse with her hair clipped at the base of her neck, responded. "Fourteen. They said it will be a while before they know if she'll make it."

The other nurse added, "She meant business. This was not an attention-getting act or a cry for help. She was checking out."

"We thought you'd want to know," Maria said.

"Of course, I do. I'm going down to the E.R. Please forward my calls," Carl requested as he rushed to the elevator and entered. He pushed the button for the right floor.

What's this going to be? I hate seeing kids and teens in such pain and desperation! And people so far out of touch with their children, Carl thought.

The elevator came to a stop, and the doors opened. As Carl exited, a lady and a little girl entered. The woman was reading a book even as she walked and seemed oblivious to the child.

"Mommy, you left your coat," the girl said.

"Yes, dear," she replied, but kept reading.

"You forgot your coat," the girl repeated.

"Oh, good," she responded, not even realizing what had been said.

Carl stopped the elevator doors from closing and motioned to the child. "Lady, will you please listen to her? People need to listen to their children. You forgot your coat," he said briskly as he shook his head and stormed off.

An intern was talking to the mother of the girl who had attempted suicide, Mrs. Mathews. Carl walked into the emergency room cubicle. Carl stood patiently and listened.

"Is she all right?" Mrs. Mathews asked.

"They've pumped her stomach and are still working on her," the intern explained. "It's helpful that we have the bottles."

Carl joined the conversation. "Bottles? Multiple? What did she take?"

"A whole prescription of sleeping pills, a prescription of Valium, and a third bottle we haven't identified. No label, but the lab's got it. Hopefully, there's enough residue to identify the medication." The intern motioned toward Mrs. Mathews. "This is Courtney's mother, Mrs. Matthews," the intern responded.

"And this is Dr. Denton," the intern said, motioning to Carl.

"Who found Courtney?" Carl asked.

"I did," Mrs. Mathews said. "She was supposed to be at school. I just happened to come home to get some reports I forgot for work."

"Do you have any idea why she'd do this?" Carl asked.

"None. I'm shocked. I can't believe it. She'll be okay, won't she? She's got to be!" Mrs. Mathews started crying.

"We will do everything possible. We've got to counteract or dilute the drugs in her system," Carl replied.

"Well, go. Do it!" Mrs. Mathews snapped.

"They are. I can assure you, she is getting the best care available," Carl stated firmly.

Judith and Becky talked in the reception area at Becky's desk. Judith thanked Becky for getting Terry and Nancy from school.

"That was a big help for you to pick up the girls. I am so grateful they want to be part of my research group. Thanks again," Judith said.

"I enjoyed getting out of the office," Becky admitted.

The phone rang. It was Paul calling for Judith. She took the call in her office.

"I found some of the legal records regarding Terry. The poor kid has needed help since she was thirteen and has not gotten it for four years. I'm surprised she is doing as well as she is. She's a mess, but it could be much worse. It's a disgrace!" Paul told Judith.

"I'm still working on any info regarding Nancy. Has she opened up to you at all? I thought you being female might help," Paul disclosed.

"Not yet," Judith said. "But she's getting more comfortable, but she's still dressing like a bag lady. It's a must that we help them both!" she acknowledged adamantly.

Judith was back in the reception area with Becky. Courageously, Becky admitted, "I saw the video you helped make. It's very good."

"Well, thank you. That's good to hear, Becky. After

Terry and Nancy finish their testing, they're going to watch it," Judith said.

"If you want to go on upstairs, I can start the video when they're ready," Becky offered.

"Great idea. Thank you again," Judith replied.

Just then, Ashley Parks entered the reception area. Judith was surprised.

"Why, Ashley, hello." Judith smiled joyously and hugged Ashley. "It's been ages since I've seen you. How are things going?"

"I need to talk to you," Ashley said.

Ashley was naturally pretty with an incredible smile and warmth. She had long, light brown hair with some golden streaks from the sun and was almost as tall as Judith. Ashley and Judith had been friends for decades. They met in middle school, even though Ashley was two years younger. Judith had helped Ashley through some extremely bad times. Ashley had learned some things the hard way.

"My office is occupied, but we can use Paul Brandon's. He's rather new here. I don't think you've met him yet," Judith replied, and they entered Paul's office.

Judith closed the door. "Is that rotten ex-husband of yours at it again?"

"No, not this time. I've gotten involved in a situation and need some advice," Ashley said.

Judith motioned to a chair, and they both sat down.

Ashley's right leg started nervously bouncing as she rubbed her hands together.

"I still work with the teenagers and kids at the rec center. Keeping them off the streets, giving them something constructive and fun to do when they're not in school," Ashley stated.

"I remember. It's a great program. I love how many of your participants' grades drastically improve with the extra tutoring you provide," Judith said, and Ashley smiled. "So, what do you need advice about?"

"There's a college student who works for me. Craig came in and announced he was quitting immediately." Ashley shrugged her shoulders. "I was surprised. He loves his job, is great at it, and it fits his school schedule."

"So, why's he leaving?" Judith asked.

"It was hard to get him to tell me, but finally, Craig told me the truth." Ashley folded her arms. "He's being pressured to have sex with Mr. Grant, the State Recreation Director."

"That's sexual harassment. Something females have been dealing with and fighting for years. It's illegal," Judith responded.

"It gets worse. Grant's in charge of all the youth programs. Everyone loves him, and he has lots of clout. Danny, the high school kid who works with Craig, came into my office to see what was happening. I'll never forget it. Danny knocked on the door and entered with his swagger. He said, 'Hey, guys, what's up? These glass walls don't give much privacy.' Craig and I looked at him and chuckled. Danny always lightens the mood.

"Then Danny continued. 'From the looks on your faces, either we're headed to a funeral, or Craig's lovely girlfriend has discovered how wonderful I am.' Craig told Danny what had happened, and then I got my second shock when Danny started again.

"'My, my. Where have you two been? I've known Grant uses his gayness since I was eight years old. Although, I must admit, I didn't know what homosexual was then.' Danny ate some candy from the bowl on the desk and began again. 'Really, I thought he was from a country named Homosex. You know, he's Japanese, he's Canadian, he's homosexual.'

"Then Craig jumped up and said, 'You knew?' Danny laughed and said, 'Kids are funny. They hear stuff and talk about it. Think they're so hot when they really don't have a clue. Once, I heard Grant got all his teeth pulled to support his habit. I thought he sold them to the tooth fairy to buy drugs. Boy, was I a dumb little kid.' Danny popped more candy into his mouth. Craig and I were stunned.

"Not only was Craig shocked, but he was a bit ticked that Danny hadn't told him about Grant. Craig asked, 'Who else knows?' and Danny responded, 'All the guys know. Grant's big thing is his basketball photos. With the pictures, he says he'll get you a scholarship or make you a star player.' Craig and I gestured our disbelief to each other.

"Danny told us more. He said, 'I met Grant and his photographer at the Rec Gym when I was twelve. They took some regular photos. Then Grant opened his briefcase and pulled out a pair of see-through pink lace undies for me to put on.' Danny shook both of his hands and continued, 'I was scared,' he said. 'I told Grant, my mom says pink is for girls, and I can't wear it. I ran home as fast as I could. The only thing I could think about was how Andrew told us how Grant took out his teeth and chased him around the locker room when he was changing clothes.' Then Danny pushed Craig's shoulder to lighten the mood.

"Danny is so funny. You'd love him. I asked if either of the guys had told their parents. Danny said, 'Are you crazy? How could we tell them that?'"

Judith listened intently. She knew Ashley was on a roll and did not want to interrupt.

Ashley shared more. "I asked if any of the boys had told any adult that Grant was tricking the boys? Danny said, 'Talking pink lace panties with anyone old enough to drive is not my style. Underneath this dynamic personality is a truly shy, sensitive soul. Besides, it isn't all a trick. Grant really does help guys get scholarships and careers.'

"I told them how that still constituted using his position for personal gain or coercion or something. I'm not a lawyer, but I know this must be illegal.

"Then Craig asked, 'You were only twelve. Isn't he over all the county teams, even the six-year-olds?'

"Danny replied, 'Yeah, he's over all the teams, and everybody loves him.'

"Craig asked, 'Why didn't I hear about Grant earlier?' And Danny responded, 'When you moved here, you were already in college. It just never came up. How was I to know that you're Grant's type? Actually, you seem a bit too old for him.'

"Then I said, What about me? I've been here for ages. Why didn't I know about this? And Danny said profoundly, 'I guess guys are embarrassed to talk about it, especially if they posed in the pink lace panties.'

"That's when I lost it. I said, Craig, you are not quitting. Absolutely, not. We'll fight this and stop it. This is an outrage!

"Then Craig pointed out, 'He'll just say we don't like gays and scream discrimination.'

"I responded emphatically, Grant being gay is not the issue. Adults can make their own choices, but adults should never involve children or teens in their sexual practices. The real problem is that Grant's a child molester and a sexual predator! That is the real issue.

"Then I asked Danny if he could get some of his friends to testify.

"Danny said, 'Maybe. The ones who didn't pose.'

And Craig said, ‘My dad's a lawyer. We'll get him to help.’”

Judith was speechless, and her mouth was agape. “Sounds like a tragic hot mess. Good thing you have a nice start.”

“That's part of the problem,” Ashley said sadly. “Craig’s parents convinced him not to tangle with Grant.”

“Why?” Judith asked.

“They feel he's too powerful politically and could damage Craig's career, and they don’t want to have to move. His mother said that gay people have their rights too. Boy, did I go off.

“Danny and Craig sat in my office, and I was standing and furious. I yelled, this is absurd. Choosing a lifestyle and sexual harassment are entirely two different issues. Not to mention possible child molestation. As a lawyer, your dad should know this. Craig just lowered his head.

“I said, Craig, you were as upset about this as I am. You need to stand up for what's right. And so do your parents.

“Danny added, ‘Hey man, she's right. And she's got a lot more to lose than we do. Her career's already here. She needs us as witnesses.’

“Craig looked at the floor and then at Danny. ‘You and your friends should be enough. You don't need me.’

“I said, Craig, he's sexually harassing you right now.

That's the easiest issue to prove.

"I am so frustrated with Craig, I could scream. And I can't believe his parents."

Judith looked at Ashley with compassion. "Some people are so full of fear that they don't stand up and never choose to do the right thing. The entire world would be a much better place if they did. It takes major courage to take a stand."

"I need the name of a good lawyer; one who can handle this whole thing. And I need advice on how to get Craig not to buckle," Ashley replied.

"Craig's in a bad position. His parents have probably given him good advice his entire life, and it's hard for him to see that they're wrong now," Judith explained. She paused and thought. "I think you should appeal to the parents first. They think they're protecting Craig, but they don't realize how damaging this will be to his inner self and affect his entire future."

"Okay," Ashley readily agreed.

"I also want you to talk to Paul Brandon. He worked in the prison system for years. He knows the loopholes and the best lawyers," Judith encouraged.

Now, Ashley did not feel so helpless and distressed. She breathed a sigh of relief and was thankful for the advice and Judith's friendship.

Carl and Judith had created a whole new council and concept almost two years ago to help children and teens. The program was still being developed but was already yielding some incredible results. Plainclothes policemen and women were spending time in all the grades of the schools. They were discreetly watching for signs of children and teens in trouble. Dirty hair, dirty fingernails, dirty clothes, bruising, avoiding eye contact, slumped shoulders, being extremely underweight, or morbidly obese, and rotting teeth were all some of the easiest things to spot.

But the real "tells" were much harder to discern and detect. Body language spoke volumes and required special training. Interaction with other students and teachers, or the lack thereof, was extremely important. Watching the eyes and the chosen stances were crucial to observe. These officers were genuinely trying to help those in trouble.

Paul loved this program because he felt they could get ahead of the problems and truly make a difference. He entered Alamance High School and walked down the hall to the door with a sign reading, Review Board in Session. Paul entered. Gina and Tom, two undercover school officers, were sitting at a small conference table waiting for their regularly scheduled meeting and discussion.

Paul surprised the two officers by getting straight to the point. "I need two arrest warrants."

"Whoa. Don't you think you've had enough scrapes with the law for one week?" Tom asked.

"We heard about what happened yesterday," Gina said with a smirk, referring to the breaking-and-entering incident and taking Katherine out of the house.

"Then you know it was right." Paul immediately responded.

"We hope for your sake that it was," Gina said seriously.

"Don't you have a hearing on it tomorrow? Isn't your position with the county on the line?" Tom asked.

"Yes, but that case has nothing to do with these two warrants." Paul placed the papers on the table. "I have a boy who's ended up in a pornography ring. And it's run by his history teacher."

"Slow down. If this is truly a porno ring, you're going to need evidence." Tom looked seriously at Paul. "If this history teacher knows you're after him, he'll destroy everything. You must play it low-key and move fast."

Paul sat down at the table. "That's good advice. I do need a plan. I want to go for the throat."

"Satisfaction follows a strong case," Tom declared.

"Wow. Wise words, Tom," Paul admitted. "That makes sense. You've been at this way longer than I have. I respect your experience and will follow your advice. And do whatever you say."

"Oh, that's going to go straight to his ego," Gina laughed. "But he is right. You said two arrest warrants.

Another teacher?" Gina asked.

"No. Gail Hall's mother leaves her with her great aunt and uncle a lot. They've filled the grandparent role for years. You're not going to believe this." Paul put his hand on his forehead. "Gail was at a retro-drive-in movie theater with her aunt and uncle. She was in the back seat, asleep. The uncle had his arm around his wife up front. When Gail woke up, the lower part of the uncle's arm was in the back, and he was fondling Gail!"

"That lousy pervert!" Gina was appalled.

Paul was furious. "Can you believe the nerve of this guy? This isn't the only incident. And Gail fully believes that her aunt knows nothing of what happened."

Tom tapped a pen against his cheek. "I imagine it's too painful for her to face. To believe her aunt would allow that." Tom scratched his head. "What I don't understand is how he could do that with the aunt right there. I know some women take part and others are silent, but right there with his arm around her? That's not only crazy but brazen. I've never dealt with anyone being so blatant unless the adult female was physically taking part."

Gina glared. "When you've been around as many years as I have, you'll see even worse. But, Paul, you need way more than that for a warrant. What you have now is simply hearsay."

Paul groaned. "I was afraid of that." He shook his head and thought. "I'm not an officer, but since Detective

Hollins is hospitalized, and you guys have me watching the high school kids the best I can for now. I have an issue and an idea. I'm great at observation, but you'd better get to the school fast if anything ever goes down. I have no authority whatsoever. And no weapon. Well, I have one, but I'm not allowed to bring it on school property." Paul pointed to himself. "It's heartbreaking to me that the teens in the worst spot are usually picked on the most. I don't want to let some teen down who needs my help. And that would technically be help, by law, I cannot provide," Paul admitted sincerely.

"Don't worry. We've got your back and can get officers there in minutes. That's why you have your beeper," Tom assured Paul.

"I'm not worried about myself. My concern is for the teens I cannot protect with no weapon! Some of these high school attacks involve multiple attackers and are brutal. The emotional damage is worse than the physical damage. No matter the severity of the attack. And they always attack those who are the most helpless and the most vulnerable.

"And forget any of the security guards being of much use. Most of the ones I've seen would run and hide. I'm headed somewhere here. I think it's worth enlisting martial arts teachers to train the weakest of the weak. As they improve, we can form them into protection groups. Strength in numbers."

Tom nodded his head. "That's a great idea for school

problems, but that does nothing for the home problems. And they are countless," Tom sighed.

Paul sighed deeply. "Tom's surveilling the middle schools." Paul looked at Gina. "You're over the elementaries. Is it bad there?"

"Yes, it is. When abuse starts so young, the children don't know any differently. They frequently think all children experience the horror they're regularly living and are so easily victimized. Their childhoods are destroyed, and often they and their futures are as well," she said sadly.

Tom responded, "That's true, but older kids and teens blame themselves more. They often feel like everything is their fault. Instead of recognizing they are victims, they think they caused the abuse, and worse, that they deserved horrific treatment. It's so tragic. The older ones are as much victims as the three-year-olds, but trying to eliminate their guilt is a monumental task. Molesters are master manipulators and experts at pouring on guilt."

Paul shook his head. "You are so right. At every age, the loss of self-esteem and trust is devastating. It affects every part of their lives and futures."

Gina got animated. "I wish we could get more adults to help. Neighbors, teachers, anybody. We need to get the message out. Molesters have had free rein for too long!"

Tom started clapping. "Bravo, bravo. You've got my

vote. I'll even be your campaign manager. Senator—no, President."

Gina laughed. "Now, seriously, some countries castrate for sexual offenses. It doesn't completely stop the abuse, but it sure is an effective deterrent." She stood up. "Men would think thrice about raping a woman if they knew the climax to the climax was a visit to the butcher!"

Tom was quite surprised and looked at Paul. Paul was shocked, as well.

Gina continued, "This is our world, our life, our country, and it will be whatever we allow and make it."

Tom smiled at Gina. "Yep! Politics. Do you get like this often?"

Paul rubbed his chin and looked at Tom. "She has a great point about the country uniting. I remember learning in one of my college classes about how the old Smokey the Bear commercials against forest fires and the drunk driving campaigns were so effective. They created massive public awareness."

"Some drunk driving awareness commercials are still running," Gina added

Tom laughed. "I can see it now, Woodsie Owl, instead of saying 'Give a hoot, don't pollute,' will look straight in the camera and say: 'If you know what's best, you won't molest.'"

Paul face-slapped his forehead and looked at Gina. "Where did you get this guy?"

"Keeping a sense of humor is an important way to hold on to your sanity in this nightmare business," she said. "And even though a commercial is a great idea, we could never do that. We don't want to be part of stealing childhood innocence!"

"Uh. Great point," Tom admitted.

Gina got somber. "We are trying to protect their innocence as much as to keep them safe from physical and emotional harm."

Terry and Nancy looked at each other in Judith's office. Terry spoke first. "This is a video you won't see at the movies or on TV."

Nancy responded, "Maybe we should. But it needs to say more, I think. They should make one for us older teens. More straight to the point."

"Yeah. They can rate it Parental Guiltiness - 13. Get it? PG-13," Terry said.

Terry pointed at Nancy. "Write that down on the evaluation. Gecco will get a kick out of that."

Judith knocked on the door. Terry responded, "Come on in."

Judith entered. "Girls, we truly appreciate your help. Would you like to come back?"

"Yeah. Will we get out of school again?" Nancy asked.

"Will 'Gecco' be here?" Terry inquired.

Judith looked puzzled. "Gecco? Oh, Dr. Brandon. Yes, he can be here, and you will get out of school early."

"Awesome. Count me in," Terry responded.

"Me, too," Nancy said.

"Great," Judith replied and looked at her watch. "It's almost six thirty. Becky's taking you out to eat, as it said on your permission slips, and then she'll drive you each home." The girls were excited. "I'll see you next week. Thank you both. Becky will be right in, and she will have your permission slips for next week. One of your parents will need to sign it in front of Becky when she takes you home."

"Bye," the girls said in unison as Judith left, closing the door behind her.

"She's pretty nice. I like her," Nancy confided.

"She's all right," Terry grumbled.

Chapter Twelve

Grasping for Hope

Mrs. Mathews was still waiting in the emergency room. She talked abruptly to the nurse. "I've been here all day with you people telling me to give it time. I want to know what's happening! What are you doing for my Courtney?" Mrs. Mathews saw an intern walking toward her. "Never mind." She walked quickly to the intern.

The intern spoke first. "We can't be positive, but things are looking better. The mystery drug was Dilaudid. All three drugs are very serious and dangerous. Frankly, considering your daughter's condition when she was admitted, it's a miracle she survived. It's a good thing you happened to go home for those reports."

Mrs. Mathews was considerably more pleasant. "Oh,

thank you. That is terrific news, at last. What a relief! Can I see her?"

"Not yet. Have you thought of anything that would have led Courtney to take this drastic step?" the intern asked.

"No. Not at all," she answered.

"Has she complained about anything? Any clue would help," the intern explained.

"Nothing," Mrs. Mathews responded with dismay.

Paul and an attractive woman were in Penny's room as Judith walked by. She assumed the woman was Penny's mother, and Judith was shocked.

"How did he get her no-good mother here? I can't believe it," Judith muttered to herself.

Judith walked to the nurses' station. "How long has Dr. Brandon been in Penny's room?" she asked.

"Umm, over half an hour," Nurse Harvey replied.

"Great. Is Dr. Denton in his office?" Judith inquired.

"No. He called about an hour ago and said he was on his way up from the E.R. I guess he got sidetracked," Nurse Harvey surmised.

Paul and the woman exited Penny's room. Judith started to walk close to Paul, then stopped.

"Thank you very much," Paul said. "You were terrific."

"I just hope it helps. She is pathetic. I feel a bit guilty

getting paid," the woman responded.

"Don't. You earned every cent," Paul said.

That's not Freda Johnson, Judith thought in surprise.

"Call if you need me again. Next time is definitely 'on the house,'" the young woman emphatically declared.

"Thanks," Paul smiled.

"Goodbye," she said as she walked toward the elevator.

"Thanks again," Paul said and waved.

Judith walked to Paul. "Who is that? I thought that was Freda Johnson."

"Let's hope that's what Penny thought," and Paul winked.

"Who is she?" Judith asked.

"An actress I hired through Buzzy Kaden. She's worked nonstop and learned as many of Freda Johnson's mannerisms as possible from that awful video," Paul said, holding up a small recording device. "And I had an electronics expert use the video to create this recording of what sounds like Mrs. Johnson's voice saying the things Penny needed to hear. It's wonderful. Now Penny's heard multiple times how nothing is her fault, there is nothing to forgive, her mother loves her dearly, and all the things her mother should have told her from the start of this nightmare." Paul sighed and smiled.

Judith was stunned. "Whoa! That was brilliant. I'm impressed. Again. Hopefully, that will open the door so

Penny can be reached. Carl will have a stroke, but I think you're a genius."

Judith hugged Paul. "This is plan A for actress, right?"

Paul laughed. "Oooooow. The fairytales were plan A, but we'll switch them just for you." They both laughed, and Paul continued, "You've been with Terry this afternoon, haven't you?"

"Yes, a delightful girl. But why does she call you Gecco?" Judith asked, and Paul chuckled. Judith shrugged her shoulders. "When I asked her, she told me to think about it, and it would come to me," Judith said.

"Well, Gecco stands for genuine cotton. Technically, genuine, one hundred percent cotton. Think about that. Terry said she added an extra c, because I'm not a geek, and she didn't want it to be a long e sound. Pretty smart, eh? I took that as quite a compliment." Paul smiled.

"What? That is a huge compliment, especially coming from a teenager. But I'm still confused," Judith stated with a befuddled look.

"What can you count on genuine, one-hundred-percent cotton to always do?" Paul asked.

Judith thought. "Be cool, wrinkle, I don't know."

Paul tilted his head to the right. "Think, now."

Judith threw up her hands. "Shrink!"

"That's right. You got it. Clever, eh?" Paul grinned.

"Very," Judith smiled.

Nurse Harvey rushed up to Paul. "Dr. Brandon, you have an emergency call on line six."

Paul hurried to the phone as Nurse Harvey yelled, "They said an extreme emergency."

Paul answered the phone at the nurses' station. "Paul Brandon." Paul listened intently. "I'll be right there. What's the address?" Paul jotted down the information. "Less than fifteen minutes."

Judith walked up to Paul as Paul hung up the phone and tore off the page where he had written the info. "I've got to go. I'll call you," Paul said, and immediately exited in a rush.

Carl walked over to Judith. "What's wrong?"

"I'm not sure. Paul got a call and had to leave," she said.

Carl walked Judith away from the nurses' station and asked, "Can you come to my office for a few minutes? I have a question."

"Of course," Judith replied, and they headed down the hall.

Judith and Carl were both seated in Carl's office. "So, what's up?" Judith asked.

"I have been wondering and concerned. I decided I needed to check," Carl admitted. "Whatever happened to the lady who unbelievably had almost a dozen guys all dazzled?" he asked quietly.

"Well, she did make it a dozen and finally got caught," Judith whispered. "It's the best thing that could have ever happened. Now, she's opened up and leveled with her husband, and he has been terrific," Judith reported. "We've added couples counseling to our visits, and I will be seeing them two or three times a week temporarily. It's a good thing my own husband, Ralph, is so understanding and supportive," Judith said.

"That's fantastic. What a relief," Carl said. "I was worried she might need some inpatient treatment. That was such a drastic and risky situation."

"I know. And riskier than she thought. She ended up with a nasty STD. At least one of the guys was playing her and pretending to be faithful, while he was actively sleeping around. However, her husband has been incredible throughout the entire ordeal.

"Out of necessity, we ramped up our sessions. It was crucial. Ralph is a sweetheart and tolerating my late nights, since it's only temporary. With the husband learning about her awful childhood and all she had been carrying and dealing with, it helps him to grasp what a mess she was and is. I am thankful she finally told him the whole truth. What a great story of true love and actual forgiveness transpiring.

"I need to tell Paul about that; he could use some good news. He's had rough cases lately, and he's working too hard. Paul needs to start dating. Better yet, he needs a wife," Judith grinned.

"Not you too. That's all I hear from Glenda. Leave the man alone. He'll get attached when he wants to. Paul's tired, but he needs sleep, not matrimony," Carl declared.

"Why, Carl, I thought you were a family man and wonderfully happy," Judith stated.

"I am. I can't imagine spending a day without Glenda. She's more precious than life itself." Carl patted Judith's arm. "But I love pecan pie too. That doesn't mean I have to shove it down everybody's throat. Besides, I don't think Paul will ever marry again."

In a small stucco house on a quiet street, a man was tied with cords to a dining room chair. A hysterical teenage boy, Robby, held a knife to the man's throat. Robby also had a rope pulled taut around the man's neck. The man was drunk and scared.

A woman sat on the couch, petrified. At the sound of knocking, a twelve-year-old girl ran to open the front door.

"Phyllis, get back here!" Robby screamed.

"No, I won't!" Phyllis opened the door, and Paul entered. "Please stop him. Don't let Robby get hurt," she pleaded.

Robby still had the knife against the man's throat. Paul carefully walked closer, with his open hands out and forward, in a non-threatening manner.

Paul spoke calmly. “Robby, please, put the knife down. Nobody's going to hurt you.”

“Who are you? And how'd you know my name?”

Paul walked slowly toward Robby. “I'm Dr. Brandon. Coach Franklin called me. He's a friend of mine. And he’s on his way here.”

Robby glared at Phyllis. “You said ya hadda go to the bathroom. You called Coach, didn't you?”

“Yes, I did. You're scaring me. I don't want you to get hurt,” Phyllis said and started crying.

“I'm not gonna get hurt, and neither are you. Not anymore. I'm sick of this fat pig pawing all over you!” Robby said, boiling over with anger.

Robby's mother squeezed her hands together. “Robby, please.”

“And you, you spineless excuse for a mother. You're always making excuses for him. You're just glad he's bothering us instead of you.” Robby mocked his mother. “‘I can't leave; we can't make it without your father!’ I hate you! I hate you both! And he's never touching Phyllis again!”

Paul agreed. “Robby, that's right. He'll never touch Phyllis or you again. Coach Franklin told me about the cuts and lashes on your back from being beaten by your father,” Paul said empathetically.

The father tried to talk, but Robby tightened the rope around his neck. He turned to Paul.

"I can take it, but I can't see him hurt Phil anymore. Or Momma."

"There's enough evidence that you and Phyllis can leave," Paul suggested.

"For where? Some foster home, where some other old lech can paw my sister? No thanks, man." Robby jerked his father back with the rope. "Or he'll convince some social worker he's terrific, and Phil'd have to come back. He ain't ever hurtin' her again!"

Robby lifted the knife to slit his father's throat. Paul yelled, "Wait!" Robby hesitated. "I know how much you love Phil," Paul said. "Coach told me he tried to get you to leave, but you wouldn't because you were worried about her." Paul gently got closer as he spoke. "Phyllis is super lucky to have you for a brother. What's going to happen to her if you kill him, and you go to jail? Who is going to watch out for her then?"

"She'll be with Momma. I don't mind being in jail if I know they're okay. Momma's not bad when he's not around," Robby said. Then he wiped his nose with the back of his left hand.

"No, Robby. It won't be good. Your mom's weak. She thinks she can't take care of you and Phil. She'll end up marrying some other lecher, just like him. There are lots of them available," Paul said with disgust. "And they're very interested in women with a child."

Robby was horror-stricken. Paul continued, "And you'll be stuck in jail, unable to help Phyllis at all. Robby, look at me."

Paul moved closer, pointing to Robby's dad. "Do you think I care what happens to this pig? I don't. The jails are full of guys just like him. I used to work in the prison system, but I had to get a different job because I couldn't stand them anymore. I did not want to help them at all. I only wanted to stop them!" Robby looked at Paul and was shocked at what he said. "If I thought you could solve your problems by knocking him off, I'd help you hold the knife. But it won't solve anything. You'll just ruin your life, and Phyllis's too."

Robby was stunned and scared.

"Please, Robby, let me help you," Paul went on. "I can take you and Phyllis away from here right now."

Phyllis cried. "Please listen to him, Robby!"

Coach Franklin came in through the front door. He gingerly walked through the foyer and toward the living room where the tense scene was playing out.

"Will we have to come back?" Robby asked with a flicker of hope.

"No. Absolutely not! You'll never have to come back. With Coach Franklin's testimony, we've got a great case. I promise," Paul declared emphatically.

Coach Franklin entered the living room. "You can come to my house, Robby. Both of you. If that's okay by the Doc here."

"Coach?" Robby asked. He was surprised to see the man, even though Paul had said Coach was on the way.

"We can arrange it. You can stay with Coach Franklin. Please, give me the knife," Paul said, reaching out his hand.

Robby started to give Paul the knife, but he hesitated.
"Give it to him, Robby," Coach instructed.

Robby took a deep breath and handed the knife to Paul. Phyllis ran to Robby and hugged him. He let go of the ropes and held her close. The emotion and love pulsed through the room. Coach was fighting back tears.

With a nod of his head, Paul silently told Coach to take the kids and leave.

"Let's get out of here," Coach Franklin directed.

Robby, Phyllis, and Coach Franklin left. Paul inconspicuously wiped the prints off the knife handle and blade with his handkerchief. Paul offered Robby's mother the knife, as he held it with the cloth, and she took the handle.

"As a legal representative of the county, I'm placing Robby and Phyllis under protective custody. You will be contacted with full details tomorrow." Paul walked to the door.

The mother put her hands on her chest. "Please, you can't take my babies. They're my babies."

Paul had his hand on the doorknob. "No ma'am,

you're wrong. I cannot take your car, your stereo, or your house, but children are not possessions or property. They have rights, and we'll see that...."

The mother interrupted Paul. "But I've never done anything to them. I love them," she said as she untied the father.

"By allowing your husband to abuse them, you have become his accomplice and are also guilty. You did nothing to stop your husband or protect your children," Paul stated firmly.

The father, having somewhat recovered, walked toward the door. "I'm pressing charges. Attempted murder, that's what it is. The world's not safe with hoodlums like that around. They'll lock him up for good. Where's that knife?"

"I gave it to your wife. But I believe if you check, the only fingerprints you'll find are hers," Paul said.

"I'll testify, you smart aleck business suit. I'll get him. Boys jail! That's where he's going."

"Why, sir, calm down. I do believe you're having alcohol-related hallucinations," Paul said.

The father grabbed his wife by the arm. "She'll testify. You'll see."

"She's so brow-beaten by you, she'd say anything you told her to. No. I'm afraid her testimony won't help your case at all. Even a first-year law school student could have her easily disqualified. You should be more worried about the child abuse charges you'll be facing.

Goodbye," Paul said and left the house.

Paul joined the other three who were waiting outside for him. They were anxious to hear what Paul had to say.

Coach Franklin asked immediately, "Could Robby really be charged?"

"Yes. He'd eventually get off, but it could be months of involvement with the juvenile authorities and a real mess. That's why I tried to stop it before it got started," Paul confessed.

"You're right. Robby needs help, not hassles. Do you think his old man will try to press charges?" Coach Franklin asked.

"No. He likes to intimidate women and children. He's not about to take us on," Paul said confidently. Then Paul smacked Coach Franklin on the shoulder, and they walked to their cars, smiling bigger with every step. Robby and Phyllis were relieved and elated.

Carl was in bed and lovingly watching Glenda brush her hair. "How do you get prettier every year?" he asked.

"I don't. Your eyesight worsens," Glenda replied. "God planned it that way."

Carl chuckled. "Oh, you beautiful lady, come here. Beautiful and smart."

Glenda got into bed beside Carl and snuggled up on his shoulder. Carl kissed the side of Glenda's head and put the covers on her.

Glenda smiled. "Your feet are cold." She rubbed Carl's feet with hers. "Doesn't this beat an electric blanket?"

"For sure, my dear," Carl said, and Glenda giggled. "Judith jumped on your bandwagon today," he said.

"Which bandwagon?" she asked.

"Getting Paul married." Carl laughed.

"Smart woman. Just think, right now poor Paul has cold feet," Glenda responded.

"In more ways than one." Carl laughed again. "He was hurt so deeply, it's going to take time."

Glenda sat up. "It's been too long already."

"It's not every day a man loses his wife, best friend, and twins all at once," Carl responded.

"Don't remind me." Extremely irritated, Glenda got up and started brushing her hair rigorously as she paced. Carl put his hands behind his head and patiently listened. "That woman should be shot. All those years, Paul stood by her when she couldn't get pregnant. Such devotion. The way he pampered her. I've never seen such a wonderful guy."

Glenda paused and looked at Carl. "Except for you, of course. Then, just when the adoption was about to go through on the twins, she left him for that creep. I don't think she ever truly wanted those children. She certainly did not deserve them. At least Paul made sure they went to a good home, since they did not want him as a single man to take them. I'd like to give her a piece of my mind!"

Carl got up and walked to Glenda. "You did," he said. "Remember?"

"Well, I'd like to do it again," Glenda replied. Carl rubbed her shoulders and kissed her head. Glenda looked at Carl. "It's been seven years, and Paul's still alone."

Carl was surprised. "Has it been that long?"

"Yes," Glenda replied.

"That's longer than I realized," Carl admitted.

"See, he does need a push," she said with a cute, flirty smile.

"A hand maybe, a push never," Carl grinned.

"Marge Griffith's niece is perfect for Paul," she stated.

"Famous last words." Carl put his hand on his forehead.

"Let's have them over for dinner," Glenda cheerfully plotted.

"That's always so strained. Couldn't we have a dinner party, so he'd have a selection?" Carl asked.

"Of course. Great idea." Glenda got excited.

"You should invite some married couples and other single men, too. So, it's not so obvious," Carl proposed.

Glenda got more enthusiastic. "Perfect! I'll start a list."

"What have I done?" Carl shook his head and kissed Glenda's cheek.

Chapter Thirteen

Do Miracles Happen?

Paul was starting a session with one of his newer clients, Sarah Bennett. Sarah was quieter than usual and seemed to be deep in thought. Paul patiently waited for her to respond.

"I'm sorry, Dr. Brandon. There is something I've been wanting to ask you. Do you believe in miracles?" Sarah timidly asked Paul.

"What do you mean by miracles?" Paul responded.

"Are you a Christian?" Sarah asked with reservation.

"Definitely, I am. Please tell me about what you are trying to share," Paul encouraged.

"Well, I've had two experiences that seem like miracles to me, and three of the people I've told agree.

But then some of the others I've shared these with warned me that I need to keep it to myself, or I might get locked away! They think it makes me sound nuts." Sarah took a deep breath.

"Were you drinking or doing drugs when these happened?" Paul asked.

"No, not at all. I never do either. With all the problems with my ex, I've always needed a clear head to keep the kids safe," she said.

"Are you being totally honest and telling the absolute truth?" Paul queried.

"Completely!" Sarah responded adamantly.

"Then, please share the facts of what happened. I truly want to hear this," Paul admitted.

Sarah looked at the ceiling for a few seconds and then began to share her experiences. "It's a long story, so bear with me, please. Although, as you know, I married my high school boyfriend and sweetheart, who treated me like a princess for years. We often talked about getting married and having children. We were engaged to be married when I was still in high school. Big diamond and all. He was older and had already graduated. But even though he had treated me like a princess for years, it ended up being a horribly abusive marriage.

"One of the counselors we tried told me he is a 'devious and evil dark Prince Charming.' Lurking behind all his sweetness and charm were sinister motives.

We've talked some about that."

Paul nodded his head and listened intently. He did not want to interrupt and remained quiet even if Sarah shared something they had previously discussed. It was important that he simply listen. Plus, he felt she needed to talk this out in her own way.

"We tried four different marriage counselors. The abuse was mostly toward me, not the children. Although occasionally he was mean to the children. I knew I had to leave, especially for the sake of my kids. They should never have been subjected to that nightmare. I wouldn't have stayed as long as I did, but each counselor thought they could fix him. But one after another, they gave up.

"My husband at the time… of course, you know, thankfully, we're divorced now. One night, he had gotten violent with me and knocked me around. I ended up on the floor, and he started kicking me severely and repeatedly while wearing combat boots. To the point where my back was in horrible shape. I couldn't walk right, and by the next afternoon, I was literally dragging my right leg.

"This is where the blessing part starts ... and the questions. When I was still with my husband, I prayed hard every day to try to save the marriage. One time, the kids and I got home after dark, and all the house lights were dim. Which was very strange because the kitchen light was especially bright. But it wasn't on as it normally was, and there was just a small light on this night. I always kept a glass of water by the sink to drink. Still do. We went into the house. I was putting groceries away, and the kids were getting ready for bed.

"I went to pick up my water glass, and a deep voice said, "Don't drink the water!" It startled and scared me. I managed to get the big kitchen light on, and the glass and water looked fine. But after that message, I didn't touch it. I had never heard a voice talk to me before that. Not ever. Later, I found a charred can in our fireplace with writing I could still read. It said odorless kerosene. My husband admitted he had filled my water glass with kerosene. He said he knew I was planning to leave him. It was so scary, and I was very thankful for the warning I had received."

"Wow! That is incredible and extremely dramatic," Paul admitted. "I've never heard a case like this. To truly be spoken to, and it turned out factually correct. That's amazing. I've studied many astonishing cases, but I've never known anyone who has had an experience. You said there were two experiences?"

"Yes. Two. I kept praying for our marriage to be saved until the last counselor we saw finally convinced me I was wasting my breath. He said he had been counseling for over twenty years and never once had he recommended divorce, until now. Then, I just prayed to do the right things for my children.

"I told the counselor I wanted to fight for the house

so my children could keep their home, and their school, and their friends. It was a nice neighborhood. Honestly, I did not want to go back there. I had too many bad memories. But I thought it would be best for the children. It didn't seem fair that they would lose all their good stuff and must start over.

"Then I got scared that maybe I was doing the wrong thing by trying to stay there. I asked the counselor if I should take the kids and go to one of those underground systems where people flee.

"He told me, 'Absolutely not!' He said that my ex was so obsessed with me that no matter how good everyone was and how hard they tried, he would find us! And he said, 'If that happens, the best-case scenario, you'd all be dead! Worst case, you'll be dead, and he'll have the kids! And heaven help those children!' He told me I had to stay and fight to keep us alive, even if that meant that the police had to come multiple times daily.

"That counselor explained more about my ex being obsessed with me. He said, 'You are his possession. Just like owning a car, he feels like he owns you. It seemed so much like love when you were dating because he was so charming and showered you with attention and gifts. Everybody probably thought you were an incredible couple. Then, even though he said he wanted kids, when you had them, that meant he had to share you. And now the kids are possessions too! He is not capable of genuine love. He is self-consumed and, honestly, only loves himself.'

"I finally left. Looking back, I can't believe I waited so long. The children and I moved in with my mom. My attorney said that with all the police reports, I could easily get the house and the divorce. However, there would be at least an eight-month waiting period to get to court, because the courts were so backed up. There was a restraining order to keep him away from us, but that only worked because the family and people around us were protecting us.

"Soon after we left, I secretly went to the hospital for testing to find out about my back and leg problems. I was living on pain medication and really struggling with my physical issues. The doctors had all the x-rays and scans showing what a mess I was. Surgery was the only solution. My mom, sister, and family kept my children while I did the necessary medical tests. Mom secretly drove them to and from school so they could at least keep that part normal. That only worked because my ex was good about going to work. He liked his job and rarely missed work. He kept threatening he was going to kidnap the children…and me too, if he could.

"Before I had full custody, my husband claimed he wanted to visit the children. The attorney said I should allow him to come if I could have several other adults there, just in case. So, he came and did his loving and charming act, which he was quite good at. He was extremely pleasant and tried to get me to go back home with him. By that time, I absolutely knew better than to fall for that routine again.

"However, when he went to leave, he quickly grabbed our son and put him in the car. He started driving away. My back and leg were killing me, but somehow I ran and jumped onto the car hood. There was no other choice. I could not have done that without God's help. I was holding onto the windshield wipers as tight as I could while he tried to buck jump me off the car. At the end of the street, he yelled out of the window that he would stop the car if I got inside. I agreed. He took us back to our house. I was petrified he would kill our son or me or both. I was in unbelievable pain, but the fear and terror overrode the absolute agony.

"Fortunately, the next-door neighbor saw what had happened. My mother called the police. When they came to my mother's house, the police determined that he had every right to take his son because I had not gotten to court yet for full custody, and that I went of my own free will. Both of those were true. So, my mother said to the police that, then they could follow her over to our house and arrest her, because she was going to go kill the—well, I won't repeat her choice words of description. My mother also called my husband's father, and he arrived at our house right after the police. He lived nearby.

"With my father-in-law there, my soon-to-be ex let us both leave. He and his dad did not get along well at all. His dad was very much on my side, and my ex was also afraid of his dad. Like most abusers, they pick on women and children. Cowards really.

"With all the medical problems I had and the proof of needing surgery, my attorney was able to get a 'show cause' hearing quickly instead of having to wait all those months to get to court. I absolutely could not be sedated until and unless I had full custody of the children, on my attorney's advice. So, I was awarded full custody at the 'show cause' hearing, along with the house.

"My husband refused to leave the house, so the sheriff and police escorted my ex out of the house. He was also given a restraining order, and the police scared him a lot. But the sheriff told me that a piece of paper would not stop an attack or a bullet. I needed a safety system if we were going to survive. He said that even if the police arrived immediately, most likely that would not be fast enough.

"So, we made a safety plan with the neighbors, and they were watching out for us constantly. All of them were great. One of the families had four boys, two in high school and two in community college, who lived at home. If their phone rang just a half ring in the middle of the night or anytime, they were immediately at our house. Everyone was incredible.

"I really am getting to the point. Eventually, I was secretly in the hospital taking betadine showers three times a day for two days to kill as many germs as possible before the operation. They were going to be doing a lot with the spine and wanted the best outcome with no complications. I had family members staying at our house and moving my car around to make it appear I was there too.

"I'm sorry this is taking so long," Sarah said.

Paul had been listening intently. "No. Don't be sorry. You are doing great. I want to understand everything. Please continue." He motioned for her to go on.

"Well, I was in the hospital, and it was almost ten o'clock at night. My operation was scheduled for seven a.m. the next morning. This may sound crazy, but this is exactly what happened. I was standing in my hospital room, and I could feel someone standing behind me, slightly to the right. Then a man's voice said, 'Go home. You will be healed.' Simultaneously, as he spoke, I got chills throughout my entire body that I had never experienced before. Then he was gone. I never saw anyone, but someone or a presence or something was there and then gone! I was stunned and frozen for a couple of minutes, not knowing what to do."

Paul was spellbound and taking in every word. He felt Sarah's sincerity and was engrossed in her story.

"Then, I picked up the phone, called my sister, and told her to quietly and quickly come pick me up. Right then. Immediately. Of course, she was shocked and asked, 'NOW? What about your surgery?' I told her

I would explain everything later, but to get there as quickly as possible. There were trusted people at the house to stay with the children while she got me.

"I started packing my stuff and buzzed for the nurse to come in. I explained I was not having surgery and was leaving. I honestly felt I needed to do what I had been told to do! The voice had been right about the kerosene. Although this was definitely not the same voice I heard before. The hospital staff had six different people come into my room at various times to try to talk me out of leaving, even bringing an E.R. doctor up from the emergency room. They all just thought I was afraid of having the surgery.

"Of course, I dared not tell them what I had experienced. I figured they'd have the hospital staff put me in a straight-jacket and move me to the psych ward. Finally, my sister arrived, and I left under much protest.

"Within three days of returning home, I was out mowing our lawn. Something I had not been able to do for over a year. My back and leg problems were gone! Completely gone! No medical explanation. My attorney assured me that everything was legally okay. Because they had the medical proof with the x-rays, scans, and tests that I was telling the truth and not faking the problems for the 'show cause' hearing. He said that without that proof, we would have had big legal problems. He also said that, legally, the children were much safer with me at home and not having a recuperation period at the hospital. I think he was almost as thankful as I was.

"Both of these circumstances feel like miracles to me! I truly thank God every day for the help I got. Prayer works. My attorney is one of the three people who believe these are miracles. That is the best explanation I can find. Either that or I am nuts," Sarah declared sincerely.

Paul sat in stunned silence for a moment. "I've read about some incredible cases regarding miracles, but you are my first patient to have experienced such remarkable events. You speak with such sincerity. What spectacular occurrences. Everything you've said is consistent with what we know is possible from the Bible.

"There are many places in the Bible where a voice spoke to someone. Moses at the burning bush. Saul, when he was on the road to Damascus, heard the voice of the risen Jesus, became a believer, and eventually was renamed Paul. There are even many instances when angels appeared and talked to people.

"I'm sorry. I got a bit carried away. My point is that what you have shared has biblical precedence."

Paul looked at Sarah. "I love your sincerity, your strength, your courage, and especially your faith. And I love your mom's daring and that she threatened to take out your ex herself. I'm going to be pondering everything you've said for a long time. Thank you for sharing your story. Sarah, I believe you. You can change your number from three believers in your miracles to four. And I am delighted to say, you are not nuts. You are extraordinary and blessed. You certainly needed some help, that's for sure, and I'm thankful you got it.

"After all you've been through, when you think about things, I wouldn't be surprised if you've had more than two miracles. What an ordeal you've endured. To answer your original question, I do believe in miracles. And if I didn't before, I would have after what you shared and experienced," Paul declared. "I wish more people would receive and recognize miracles."

Sarah gave a deep sigh of relief. "Thank you. That is wonderful to hear. My attorney does think I had a third miracle. I kept praying for the best for my children. And from the time I took the kids and left, it was only forty-five days until we were back home, and I was mowing the lawn. He said that with his legal experience and knowledge, only a miracle could have accomplished that so quickly. My attorney also believes that us having the legal medical proof that we needed is a fourth miracle. But I'm not sure if those were miracles since there was no voice involved, or answers to prayers."

Paul gestured with both hands. "Wow again! Either way, you had divine help! Thankfully. We all need more belief, recognition, and appreciation of the help we do receive. You've done a remarkable job facing awful trials and keeping your faith.

"Corrie Ten Boom, who survived an evil and awful WWII Nazi concentration camp, is one of my heroes. Technically, she would be a heroine. I love two of her quotes. She said, 'Happiness isn't something that depends on our surroundings; it's something we make inside ourselves.'

"She also gave an amazing quote that I believe is quite fitting for now. It totally fits what you have experienced. Corrie said, 'Faith sees the invisible, believes the unbelievable, and receives the impossible.'"

Chapter Fourteen

Facing Truth Is Often Hard

Mr. Hutchenson was walking out of Judith's office. "See you next week," he said.

"Good-bye," Judith responded. Judith looked at Paul's dark office and turned to Becky. "It's ten thirty. Where is Dr. Brandon?"

"He was here earlier but is gone now. Remember? I'm not supposed to know, but that hearing is today." Becky said.

"Oh, no! I can't believe I forgot. Please cancel my appointments and handle things here. I'm going to the hearing. Just say that something came up and offer my apologies. I'll be here this afternoon and will work late if anyone needs an appointment today." Judith wrote a note and handed it to Becky. "Please give this to Ashley Parks when she comes. Thanks." Judith left, and the telephone rang.

"Doctors Ramsey and Brandon." Becky gave her usual greeting, then smiled. "Dr. Brandon's working late tonight alone, and I'm not missing my chance. I've got the whole thing planned."

The hearing room was bustling with people and papers. Various men and women were all seated. Carl sat at the very back. Paul faced the panel as he was being questioned, so he did not see that Carl was there.

"Dr. Brandon, even though this is just a hearing, you are still under oath and required to tell the truth."

Judith entered. She saw Carl and sat beside him. "Hi. Does Paul know we found out about this?" Judith whispered.

"No. That's why I'm back here," Carl said.

"How's it going?" Judith asked.

"Not well, I'm afraid. You know Paul, he won't defend himself," Carl huffed.

"Yeah, that let-them-think-what-they-like attitude is going to do him in," Judith concluded.

"And the school program, if he's not careful," Carl strongly stated.

"Now, Dr. Brandon, Ms. Harman testified that your

actions were heroic and commendable. However, the question is, were they necessary?" Lawyer Conway grilled Paul.

Conway motioned to the panel. Ms. Harman stood up. "He is a hero," she shouted.

"You've already testified," Conway said rudely. "Remain seated." Harman reluctantly sat down.

Conway glared at Paul. "I feel your actions were totally out of line. In fact, it appears you sent Ms. Harman to get the police so she wouldn't stop you. At all times, did you remember you were representing the county in your actions? And if you had it to do over again, what would you do?"

Carl looked at Judith. "This guy's been watching too much television."

"As I previously stated, I do not regret my actions. Faced with a similar situation, I would act accordingly," Paul stated clearly.

Conway began to pace and glare. "You have nothing further to add?"

"No. The child's welfare must always be the main concern," Paul explained.

"Considering we have a possible breaking-and-entering charge, assault and battery, and child abduction, I motion to suspend Dr. Brandon pending further investigation."

Carl, extremely shocked, looked at Judith and jumped up. "Sirs, I would like to address the panel. I have some pertinent information."

The panel members were talking among themselves. Paul mouthed to Carl, "What are you doing here?"

Carl mouthed back and smiled, "Trying to address the panel."

Paul did not want to get Carl involved in any trouble. Paul started to object, but Carl stopped him with a look and a hand motion. Carl also mouthed, "Not a word, please."

The chairman of the hearing spoke to Carl. "Dr. Denton, we all recognize and respect you greatly. However, we are also aware of your friendship with Dr. Brandon."

Carl responded, "I'm not here to deliver a testimonial. I only plan to state facts."

The chairman looked at the other panel members. They each nodded with approval.

"Please, the floor is yours," the chairman responded.

"Dr. Brandon acted correctly in every aspect of his behavior. He should be commended."

The chairman objected. "Dr. Denton, please . . .."

Carl put his hand up in a stop motion. "Bear with me. I need to relate the facts of a similar situation that Dr. Brandon was involved with many years ago. This was before he was a full-fledged doctor."

Judith gave Carl an approving smile. She put her hand to her chest and struggled to fight back tears.

Carl rubbed his neck. "The situation was relatively

similar. Child sexual abuse was suspected. The father was in the house with his daughter and refused to open the door. In this case, the doctor, against Paul Brandon's advice, stayed off the property and waited for the police."

The chairman impatiently rolled his eyes. Then he looked at his watch.

Carl took a deep breath. "While the doctor waited for the police, the father slipped out of the back door with his daughter, borrowed a car from a neighbor, and got away."

"You say that was against Dr. Brandon's advice; he must have waited all these years to do it his way," the chairman said sarcastically.

"If that was the case, then, thank heaven he did. That thirteen-year-old girl was found dead the next day. She had been violently raped and severely beaten by her father."

Judith wiped tears from her face and eyes. She battled not to cry harder, as Carl continued.

"Now, that doctor in charge did everything legally right. Not one claim or charge could be brought against him. But it was at the expense of a girl's life."

The chairman glared at Carl. "It seems extremely convenient that you happen to be here, and Dr. Brandon just happened to have related this story to you."

Carl strongly pointed his finger at the chairman. "I purposely came because I knew Paul would not tell you this factual occurrence. Paul had no idea I would be here."

"Well, it still seems awfully convenient," the chairman snidely replied.

Carl gritted his teeth and squeezed a fist. "No. 'Convenient' is not a word related to this situation whatsoever. You referred to Paul as having related this story to me." Carl looked at each panel member. "Paul never told me about this; he never had to. I was the doctor in charge who waited for the police that night."

The room became completely silent. The panel members were flabbergasted and looked at each other.

Carl continued, "You can be legally right and morally wrong. Dead wrong in my case, and that is something I must live with every day for the rest of my life," Carl said as he fought back tears.

A cold stillness filled the room. The panel member to the left of the chairman spoke. "I move we forget this nonsense and support Dr. Brandon."

"I second that motion," the panel member to the right of the chairman said forcefully.

The chairman hesitated. "All in favor?" he asked sheepishly.

A resounding "AYE" came from each member.

"This hearing is adjourned," the chairman said.

Paul went straight over to Carl, and they hugged. Paul said, "Carl, you . . .."

Carl interrupted. "Should have done exactly what I

did. You'd have done the same thing." Carl smiled.

"Thank you," Paul said and hugged Carl again.

Judith walked over to them. "Come on, guys. I'll treat you both to lunch."

Carl patted Paul's back. "She's made us an offer we can't refuse. Let's go eat."

They walked out of the room, and Carl hesitated with a grin. "Now this doesn't mean you're right about everything. I heard about that actress stunt, and I do mean stunt. I wasn't too thrilled, and Penny's condition has not changed one bit."

"I didn't think it would yet," Paul replied immediately. "I'm just hoping this will help her be able to respond."

Judith changed the subject. "Hey, guys. Mexican? Indian? French? What sounds good? You name it."

"Whatever's closest and fastest. I need to get back to the hospital," Carl said.

Ashley came down the hall, and Judith walked to meet her. "You got my note," Judith said.

"Yes. Are you all right?" Ashley asked.

"Oh, yes. You know Carl," Judith said as she turned to Carl.

Carl opened his hands toward Ashley as he gestured. "You look wonderful. You've recovered well from all that garbage you had to deal with. Good to see you."

"Well, thank you, sir. And you're as handsome as ever," Ashley smiled.

Judith motioned to Paul. "And this is Paul Brandon.

He's the one I want you to talk to." Motioning to Ashley, Judith said, "Paul, this is Ashley Parks. She's the one who needs your advice."

Ashley put out her hand, and they shook. "Hello, Paul."

"Nice to meet you," Paul said.

"We're on our way to lunch. Can you join us?" Judith asked.

"Oh, I'm sorry. I can't. I have an appointment," Ashley said regretfully.

"Rats. You need to talk to Paul as soon as possible," Judith reminded her.

"I know," Ashley agreed.

"I'll be working late tonight. Could you come by my office any time after eight?" Paul asked.

"That's perfect," Ashley replied, then looked at the time on her phone. "I'll see you tonight. Nice to meet you, Dr. Brandon. I've got to run. I'm late. Bye, everybody." Ashley waved as she turned to leave.

"Nice to meet you too," Paul replied.

"Bye," Judith called.

"I've always liked her," Carl said.

"Me, too," Judith replied.

"Oh, Glenda's hosting a dinner party Sunday, and she wants you both and Ralph there," Carl announced.

"We'll be there," Judith committed.

"You too, Paul," Carl smiled.

"I'll try," he said.

"He'll be there," Judith stated unequivocally.

Paul was writing at his desk. The door was open, and Judith entered.

"Are you working all weekend?" Judith asked.

"Probably. It's been a busy week," he admitted.

Judith closed the door and sat down. "Do you have any new ideas to try to help Penny?" she asked. "We're desperate."

"I thought of one that I don't think would hurt, and the change might help," he said.

"At this point, anything's worth a try," Judith responded.

"Well, Ben told me that Penny loves to sit in the pool," Paul shared.

Judith's eyes got big. "Uh, I don't know how Carl would take that. A small swimming pool set up in her room?" Judith grimaced.

"There's no other choice. The only way to try it with the I.V. is to do it in her room. Also, the monitor disconnection will be briefer there. And I think trying the pool is worth a shot. Something totally different yet familiar. Hopefully, Carl will understand," Paul replied.

"I hope," Judith said with her fingers crossed and nodding her head. She paused. "Well, we could try it without telling Carl. That eliminates the problem and keeps him totally innocent. Plus, it will be for a short time, and it truly seems worth doing."

Paul hesitated. "It will be very visible, so I think Carl will see it."

"Oh well, at least we have a plan?" She looked at Paul.

Paul smiled. "Hhhmmm. We've got to at least try it. We're desperate. So, yes!"

"Oh, good. It feels terrific to have some hope again," Judith admitted.

"You are right about that," Paul agreed.

Judith got excited. "Hey, we've got some time, so tell me why you left the prison system. I've been wondering about that and waiting to hear," Judith encouraged.

"Oh, that," Paul replied.

"Yes. I've been dying to know, and you promised," she reminded Paul.

Paul pointed to the two-way mirror. He asked, "Anyone there?"

"No. Everybody's gone," Judith assured Paul.

Paul was hesitant, but Judith prodded him. "So, come on. Tell already."

One big sigh and Paul began. "I should probably preface this by explaining that I believe, as human beings, we all make mistakes. And, if we do not learn from those mistakes, we are destined to repeat them. That's true of people and, also, countries and governments."

"I agree with that totally," Judith admitted. "Well said. Please continue."

"For decades, I enjoyed living in Maryland. It was close to all the fascinating things in D.C., especially the Smithsonian. But then the crime became bad, shootings and all.

"I worked in the worst prison in Maryland. Lots of gang violence, murderers, and repeat offenders, among others. It was the Maryland Correctional Institution in Hagerstown. Originally, I planned to make a difference for those who had regrets and wanted to change. I tried for years to help the prison inmates. When an inmate wanted to change, that was easy. But most of them didn't want to change."

"That's sometimes true of patients, too," Judith admitted.

"Yeah, but I started feeling like almost all the inmates didn't want to change. They only didn't want to get caught the next time," Paul declared. "There was little or no sincere remorse for the terrible things they had done."

"That would be discouraging," Judith said.

"You may have noticed the quote on my wall from Aleksandr Solzhenitsyn. 'Do not pursue what is illusionary—property and position…prize above all else in the world those who love you and who wish you well,'" Paul said, pointing to the framed quote.

"I have, and I love that quote," Judith said. "Although

I must admit I don't know much about the guy who wrote it. History was my worst subject."

Paul chuckled. "Oh, I'm a bit of a history buff, and Solzhenitsyn is one of my favorites. What courage he had his whole life. He was a young Russian soldier during Stalin's rule of his country. Solzhenitsyn recognized some of the horrible things Stalin was doing and wrote a letter stating how things should be better, not knowing the government read all the mail. He was sentenced to eight years in a Russian Gulag for that letter. What they did to the people and the prisoners was horrific and beyond cruel. Solzhenitsyn listened to many of his fellow inmates share stories of what they and their families had tragically suffered and endured. He memorized their experiences and spent his life making people aware of the truth. Stalin killed at least twenty million of his Russian citizens. Maybe even up to sixty million.

"Like his friend, Hitler, Stalin was evil and sadistic! Solzhenitsyn wrote volumes of books letting the world know the truth about the evil that was perpetrated against his people and humanity.

"With all of Solzhenitsyn's writings, he said he could not sum it all up as well as some of the older Russian people had done when they tried to figure out the why of what had happened to them and their country. What they concluded and said was, 'Men have forgotten God; that's why all this has happened.'

"I think there is such truth in that statement that everyone should remember it," Paul said adamantly. "We all need our Father in heaven and His Son, Jesus Christ, in our lives daily. It is so important that we don't forget that, because if we do, I think we will regret that decision, that action, more than any other of our whole lives. Simply, because that huge mistake will lead you to many more mistakes before you realize what has happened. It will ultimately cause you more regrets in your life than any other decision or choice you ever make. More than people ever imagine.

"So, I commissioned that piece of artwork on the wall hanging next to Solzhenitsyn's quote that I brought from my office at the prison. It is a reminder of what Solzhenitsyn's people concluded about what happened when they forgot God. The quote about God is written on the back of the painting, as a reminder to me never to forget God or Jesus. If I thought someone was open to God, I let the prison chaplain know who they were."

"I've always wondered about that picture," Judith admitted. "I was going to ask about it someday. I don't get it."

Paul pointed to the picture toward the top. "This is a beautiful mountain range somewhere in Russia. If you look closely at the tallest mountain peak, you'll see the number twenty million with two plus signs, representing the Russian civilians killed by Stalin's evil actions. I like to think that all their remains have been buried by now,"

Paul stated somberly, and sighed.

"On a side note, you cannot study history in depth without learning that evil is quite real! And present at least on one side in every war. Sometimes both sides. Evil utilizes power, ambition, insecurity, greed, et cetera, as weapons and tools of manipulation. Well, and all the deadly sins. But it is more than selfish human nature behind the Hitlers and Stalins of the world. Evil is very real! I digress. Remind me to tell you something about Hitler I think you'll find interesting. But back to the painting."

"This is fascinating," Judith encouraged.

Paul smiled and pointed to the artwork again. "In the separate section across the bottom, the Roman numeral one is for World War I, the Roman numeral two is for World War II, then the large G on top of the large F is for God Forbid, followed by Roman numeral three for—what I pray never happens—World War III. And everyone should pray it never happens."

Judith was impressed. "Why, Paul, how creative. I always thought those were prison bars. The way the Roman numerals have a line on the top and bottom, and are arranged so close together, it makes them look like a prison cell."

Paul smiled. "That was intentional. Good catch. The quote about, 'Men have forgotten God' (and women have too) is true of almost every prisoner I worked with. Not all, but most. When I started working at the prison,

I hoped to gently remind a few prisoners about God and the faith that, perhaps, they once had. That's why I had the picture made. To remind me not to forget that.

"Wars and crimes trade God's beautiful creations and gifts to us for prison walls! It happens repeatedly. Some prisons are made of bars, and some are made of broken emotions. But many are made by selfish choices. People were not created for jail cells. They were made for glorious good--beautiful mountains and the grandeur of the world. And the caring for and serving of one another. It is the evil and the horrible choices people embrace that make jail cells a necessity and emotional prisons a reality.

"But by the time I left the prison system, it had been proven to me that, unfortunately, most of the prisoners had embraced evil and should stay right where they were. Concerning many prisoners, the world and innocents are safer with them behind bars. There were some exceptions, but very few.

"The bragging got to me more than anything. They'd brag about the people they'd hurt or killed. Old people, children, women, men. It was terrible." Paul got progressively more emotional. "One man had killed his girlfriend. His biggest regret was that he could no longer molest her ten-year-old daughter. And the mother knew what he was doing! She allowed it. It made me sick."

Judith was stunned. She remained silent, listening intently, not wanting to interrupt.

"I stopped trying to delve into the causes of their actions. I decided most of them were just rotten people who had done what they had wanted to do. They had embraced the evil side, which God warned us about." Paul stopped and shook his head. "I didn't care anymore about helping them; I just wanted to stop them."

Judith's eyes widened. "No wonder. That had to be awful."

Paul continued, "I realized I wasn't doing anyone any good, me included. So, I decided to work on the other side of the gate, preventing some of these crimes and situations from happening. I was so burned out and disgusted that I truly wanted to leave the state, as well. And for other reasons. So, I picked beautiful North Carolina, where it's not far to drive to the mountains or the beach. There are terrific universities and a bounty of research and development operations that I find interesting. I considered moving farther west, but I like having the East Coast greenery and all the seasons."

Paul paused. "Truthfully, there is a bit more to how I picked North Carolina. I started with my nephew's puzzle map of the United States. You know, where each piece is a state. I made a pile of yeses, nos, and maybes. Originally, North Carolina was in the no pile. I had been there when I was in elementary school and hadn't had such a good time. I visited various 'yes' and 'maybe' places, but none worked for me. Then, when I was totally desperate, I finally did what I should have done at the beginning. I prayed about where I should move. I got a very strong feeling to take North Carolina out of the no pile." Paul laughed. "I should have prayed at the start of my quest. It sure would have saved me a lot of time and money." Paul tried to lighten the mood. "So here I am, end of story."

"That's an incredible experience about how you ended up here! You are such a great example to me about trying and relying on prayer. That's an amazing lesson for all of us and an excellent move. I'm glad you got out of that prison program. It sounds like you were burned out with great cause. But you learned a lot," Judith said.

"A lot I wish I didn't know." Paul sighed deeply.

"It will eventually pay off. It already has. You are remarkable." Judith smiled.

"You're sweet. Oh, and something you may not know. When I took the NC puzzle piece out of the no pile and looked at it, the first person I thought of was Carl. We've been friends for many years. When I was attending Georgetown University in D.C., Carl was a guest speaker for one of my classes. My professor introduced us. We clicked right away and have been friends ever since. That's how I got here," Paul admitted.

"No wonder you two seem so close," Judith responded.

There was a knock at the door. Paul jumped.

"That must be Mrs. Deganti," Paul said and quickly

walked toward the door.

"I need to go anyway. Don't work too late," Judith said as she walked.

Paul opened the door. "Come in, Mrs. Deganti. This is Dr. Ramsey."

The two women nodded pleasantly. "Good night," Judith said and left.

"Mrs. Deganti, please, have a seat," Paul directed.

"I'm a little nervous," she confessed.

"That will pass quickly," Paul encouraged her.

"I hope," Mrs. Deganti admitted.

"On the phone, you said you needed to talk to me regarding the two girls you nanny," Paul recapped.

"Yes. My friend told me you are super, so that's why I'm here. I started to do something months ago, but I was afraid to get involved. So, I convinced myself nothing was happening," she confessed.

Mrs. Deganti rubbed her arm and looked away from Paul. "I've made up all sorts of excuses for things I've seen, but I can't keep doing that. Something needs to be done. I think," she said hesitantly.

"Tell me about what you've seen. How old are the girls?" Paul asked.

"Alice is seven, and Karen is five. I've noticed many little things that weren't right, until now. I hope my keeping quiet didn't make things worse." Mrs. Deganti began to wring her hands.

"Take some deep breaths," Paul suggested, and

paused. “What’s happened?” he asked.

“The girls were playing. They were on the floor, then Alice partially got on top of Karen. She started touching her private parts. I called them over to look at my knitting and asked what they were playing.”

Mrs. Deganti hesitated. Paul sat quietly and waited.

She began again. “Alice said she was pretending to be her ‘daddy,’ and Karen was pretending to be Alice. I even questioned that and asked, ‘Don't you mean your mommy?’ They both insisted she was Alice.” Mrs. Deganti rubbed her hands frantically. “I was shocked. I didn't ask questions. I just told them to play with their toys. But today Alice complained about problems with her private parts. I didn't know what to do. I don’t know what to do.” She began to cry.

Paul offered Mrs. Deganti the tissue box from the side table, which was a must-have in their offices. She took several tissues.

“I'm glad you came,” Paul stated. “These children need help. Could you possibly take Alice to her pediatrician as soon as possible?”

“Yes. I thought about that. I should have done that today.”

“Let's try that first,” Paul suggested. “The pediatrician should take it from there. That’s the fastest and best route. Hopefully, that's all you'll need to do. If not, we will continue with other measures. These children are lucky to have you on their side. I will help you with every needed step for the entire journey."

Judith sat in her car and pondered. She wondered if the "And for other reasons" Paul referenced for wanting to leave Maryland was his divorce.

Chapter Fifteen

Oh Dear!

Carl and Glenda were having a nice candlelit dinner in their dining room. Glenda looked romantically at Carl. Carl was not expecting what followed.

"It's all arranged," Glenda said and grinned. "We're having four single men, four single women, Judith and Ralph, and us. Doesn't that sound perfect?"

"It does. I'm glad you kept it simple. I was prepared for a marathon of unmarried people parading through our house." Carl laughed.

"Oh, Carl."

"Did you invite Ashley Parks?" he asked.

"No. Remember, you told Judith and me a year ago to stop trying to get Ashley paired up. Besides, she's determined not to remarry until her children are grown, if ever, which I don't blame her for. They've been through too much already," Glenda said emphatically. "With her husband literally trying to kill her!"

"Well, can't she just come to eat? It would be good for her to get out," Carl suggested.

"But I don't readily know another nice available male."

Carl chuckled. "Oh dear, they must come in sets, I suppose."

Glenda gave Carl a dirty look. Then she focused on cutting her steak.

Carl smiled. "I could always put a notice on the bulletin board at the hospital. 'Attention all bachelors, willing to surrender said title.' We can place it right under, 'Needed: lab rats.'"

"Oh, you!" She grinned.

"Just kidding," Carl said, and took Glenda's hand in both of his. "I sure do love you."

Glenda touched Carl's face. "I sure do love you, too. I wish everyone could have the happiness we share," she said. "We have so many friends with great careers, who aren't happy because they're alone."

Carl smiled. "No matter how fulfilling your work is or how much you love your job, it can never make up for not having a connected, loving relationship."

Glenda looked at Carl lovingly. "I love you so much. And I love us! You are right. Even though some of our friends are married, they're worlds apart from each other. They're not connected like we are."

"Yeah. But not everyone was lucky enough to live next door to old Mr. Woodrum." Carl laughed.

"That's true." Glenda nodded and chuckled.

Carl gestured toward Glenda with his hand. "He preached to me for years. 'No amount of success can ever make up for a failed marriage.'

"I can still hear him. 'Put your family first and everything else will be fine.'" They laughed.

Carl shook his finger. "If I worked late a few times, he'd meet me at the car." Carl imitated Mr. Woodrum. "'Working late can't be helped sometimes, but it can be made better. Dinner, a movie, flowers, something. Women ought not to be taken for granted.'"

Glenda raised her glass. "What a wise and caring man he was. To Mr. Woodrum."

Carl followed Glenda's lead and raised his glass. They clinked glasses and drank a toast to Mr. Woodrum and his wisdom.

Glenda reminisced. "When I was so involved with that school carnival, he made certain I sent you love notes and fixed your favorite meals."

They clinked their glasses again and offered another toast. Glenda stated, "It's good we're drinking our homemade prickly pear lemonade. Instead of getting drunk, we're getting healthy and saving our brain cells. And we can thank Mr. Woodrum for that, too."

Carl laughed. "After the last board meeting, the chairman asked me what I attributed my success to, and I told him, 'Mr. Woodrum.'"

Glenda took a bite of her dinner.

Carl continued, "After explaining about Mr. Woodrum, the chairman said he wished he had known him. It took him three divorces before he realized that a good marriage isn't magic but lots of effort and thoughtfulness."

"Mr. Woodrum should have been a marriage counselor," Glenda suggested.

"Nah," Carl said. "Nobody ever listens to them." They both laughed.

Glenda became serious. "In reality, with all the people we know who are divorced, I think Mr. Woodrum was our guardian angel."

Paul was working at his desk. Becky entered his office in a full-length evening gown and carried a picnic basket.

"I saw Mrs. Deganti leave," Becky said and smiled.

Paul was surprised. "Why, Becky, what are you doing here?"

Becky pulled a blanket from the basket. Then she placed the basket on the table and spread the blanket on the floor.

"I knew you were working late, so I brought dinner," Becky said happily.

Becky knelt on the blanket. She gave Paul a romantic look as she removed items from the basket to the blanket. Paul was irritated but composed himself.

"I appreciate the thought, Becky, but I've already eaten," Paul stated emphatically.

"You can at least have dessert," Becky smiled. "I'm not taking no for an answer."

"Becky, that wasn't my last appointment," Paul explained.

"It's my job to schedule the appointments. I know that was the last one," Becky confidently replied.

"Officially yes, but I have a consultation scheduled that may take hours. I'm expecting Ms. Parks any moment," Paul declared. He leaned down and put items from the blanket back into the basket. "Let me help you get things put back. I'm sure you can share this nice dinner with one of your friends."

Becky reached up and kissed Paul. Paul quickly removed Becky's arms from around his neck.

"Miss Perkins!" Paul said harshly.

At that same moment, Ashley appeared at Paul's door. She was stunned and did not know what to do. Ashley paused and looked around. "Oh, excuse me," she said. Ashley was embarrassed and quickly tried to leave.

Paul rushed after her. "Ms. Parks, wait, please," he

called. "Don't leave."

Becky was frustrated and angry that her plan had not worked. She began throwing things into the basket as fast as she possibly could.

Paul stopped Ashley Parks from leaving right outside his office. “Please come in. I’ve been expecting you.”

Ashley hesitated. “I can come back if I’m rushing you.”

Paul spoke directly to Ashley. “Oh no. Now is a fine time. Miss Perkins was just leaving.”

Becky angrily grabbed the basket she had just repacked and stormed to the door. “Yes, I was just leaving!” she stated bitterly and then attempted to calm herself. “How long did you say you’d be?”

“Hours,” Paul replied. “Have a nice weekend. We’ll see you on Monday.”

“Maybe before,” Becky said.

Paul was emphatic, “No. Good night.”

Becky glared at Paul and huffed off.

Paul’s eyes widened. “Ms. Parks, please come into my office.” They entered the office, and Paul closed the door. “Please have a seat,” he said to Ashley.

“In the chair or on the floor?” Ashley smiled as she realized what had just transpired.

Paul shook his head and motioned to the chair. “Please.”

Ashley grinned. “I must say, you have some very unique counseling methods.”

Paul immediately responded. “Miss Perkins is not my patient; she’s our temporary receptionist.”

“O-O-Oh. That’s right. I didn’t recognize her. Well then, you have unique employment practices.”

“She just . . ..” Paul sighed in frustration. “Never mind. Judith filled me in on what you told her.”

“Oh, good. I’ve been thinking. Robert, that’s one of the guys pictured on Grant’s Wall of Fame,” Ashley paused and then explained. “Those are the guys that Grant helped through high school and college.” Ashley was struggling to describe what she suspected. “Well, he’s Grant’s assistant, but he’s often rude to Grant and won’t let his son go anywhere near Grant without him. I always thought Robert was just an ingrate, but now I understand.”

“Tough spot,” Paul said.

“I’m hoping Robert will testify. Any ideas that will help?” Ashley asked.

“From what you’ve said, he’s openly hostile. But it will depend on what he’s willing to admit happened. That can be tricky, especially since he has a son. I’m sure there are things he doesn’t want his son to know. And he might even have other kids,” Paul said.

“Oh, dear. That would be hard. Very hard,” Ashley agreed.

“Seems like Robert has been around Grant for a long time. You may want to arrange a legal offer of immunity for Robert. In case he was present when Grant was inappropriate with a minor. That will help him to talk more freely. It sounds like he's a former victim protecting his son. And stuck because he needs his job." Paul shook his head. "From what I've heard, Grant has tons of pull and countless connections. This will be a tough battle." Paul looked disturbed and scratched his head in thought.

"Would you help me talk to Robert?" Ashley asked. "I think it will go better if you do."

"Of course," Paul agreed.

"Also, I'm hoping you can recommend a good lawyer. I haven't a clue," Ashley admitted.

"That's super important. Grant's going to claim homosexual persecution and tout gay rights, trying to cloud the issue of child molestation—two completely different situations. Adults can make their own choices. But honestly, I get sick and tired of seeing children and teens have their childhoods stolen by self-centered perverts! Children being used for and abused for self-gratification is more than a crime; it's evil. That's the worst kind of evil. Often, not only are their childhoods stolen, but their whole lives often end up in tragedy without some help. There is a huge list of horrible outcomes." Paul stopped and took a deep breath. "I'm sorry. Some of these situations make my blood boil."

"I appreciate your compassion and that you care so much. It's impressive," Ashley sincerely said.

Paul was somewhat embarrassed by compliments

and moved straight back to the facts. "The best way to eliminate or help avoid one major problem we face is for you to have a gay, male attorney. One that is appalled by child molestation and what Grant's done."

"Of course. That's a fantastic idea." Ashley started to feel hope.

Paul continued. "There's a big difference between being a homosexual and being a pedophile. I know we can find the right lawyer. I have a couple in mind."

"Terrific. This is the first sense of relief I've felt in weeks," Ashley confessed. "I'll check with Robert to see when he's available and let you know."

"That sounds good. We've got a plan," Paul smiled. He was also feeling some relief after his emotional outpouring.

"Thank you so much for seeing me. I already feel much better. I appreciate it more than you know." Ashley stood and offered her hand to Paul. They shook hands, smiling.

"Any time. Don't hesitate to call. We can do this. I have to say, I appreciate your courage. Keep up the good work. Standing up for the right thing is not always easy, but there is nothing more imperative," Paul said.

Ashley blushed and changed the subject. "It didn't take us as long as I thought it would. Maybe Miss Perkins is still around."

Paul realized Ashley may be right. Ashley started to leave.

"Do you think Robert might be available tonight?" Paul suggested.

Ashley was surprised. "It's worth a try. Let's find out."

"We should act on this as soon as possible," Paul said. He quickly grabbed his coat.

"But don't you have plans?" she asked.

"Just paperwork. It can wait," he answered.

"All right, let's go." Ashley was excited to be getting help.

Chapter Sixteen

Use Logic to Override Emotion

It was a beautiful night. Paul and Ashley sat on her porch swing. They admired the stars in the clear night sky. "I can't believe it's two a.m. I feel like I haven't stopped talking. Please take a turn," Ashley requested.

"You amaze me," Paul admitted. "Your children seem more well-adjusted and accomplished than any I've ever seen. How have you done that with all the garbage you had dumped on you?" Paul asked. He genuinely wanted to understand.

"There you go again, turning it back to me," Ashley pointed out.

"Seriously, I want to know. Seeing you so successful and your kids doing so well gives me hope. My interactions are mostly with people who are struggling. Please, share." Paul encouraged Ashley to answer.

Ashley looked at Paul. "Don't sell yourself short. Good counseling is crucial. It was that one counselor who helped me understand that my sister, who was so physically abusive and mean to me, set me up for the mistreatment from my ex. I remember being only four years old, and she was in middle school. You see, all my sisters were from my mom's first marriage and much older than I was. Well, she would make me stand in the bedroom or bathroom and let her scratch places on my arms until they bled. Blood would be dripping, and I would be crying. Then, she'd get scared she was going to get in trouble. She'd start saying how sorry she was and how much she loved me! And, of course, 'Please don't tell.' It was horrible! Once she beat me with a wire coat hanger. Another time, she beat me with pop beads. They were like a plastic rope. I had welts all over me, including my face. She got in trouble for those two, even though I didn't tell, my mother could not help but see the injuries on me, especially my neck, cheeks, and forehead. However, my sister never got in enough trouble that she stopped hurting me. When I look back on it, I cannot believe my mother allowed it!

"Then, I ended up in the same type of relationship with my abusive husband, even though he started as Prince Charming. He was going to protect me and keep me safe. That didn't last. The counselor helped me to understand that if someone hurts you, that is not love. Even if they say they love you a thousand times! Which should be common sense, but it's not when you are damaged at such a young age.

"If someone really loves you, they will be good to you! The 'I'm sorry' and 'I love you' do not make up for the abuse, no matter how many times they are said! They only program you to hope they are sincere statements. And especially when they happen when you are young, they program you to accept the abuse as normal. Although I've known people who had good childhoods who got caught in a web of abuse, as well."

Paul's heart ached for all Ashley had endured. "I am so sorry you were subjected to such cruelty and violence! And it angers me not only that your older sister would treat you that way, but that your mother would allow such abuse. It is beyond horrific. I'm thankful that the counselor was able to help you understand that love is an action, and not just a word! To way too many people, it is just a word with little or no true meaning."

"Boy, do I understand that. Finally! All my kids do too. When we say it, we mean it!" Ashley said.

Paul smiled. "And that is very apparent. I can even feel the love you and your children emanate. You have such a caring family. You've done a fantastic job!" Paul acknowledged.

"Thank you," Ashley smiled. "I never wanted to be anything like my sisters, especially the worst one, and thankfully, I'm not. Dr. Cline said that sometimes people who are abused become abusers. But ironically, my ex was never abused. He was just sadistic and enjoyed hurting others and inflicting pain. I didn't know it, but my ex even abused animals when he was a child. Apparently, that's a horrible sign and indicator."

"Yes, it is!" Paul declared. "You are amazing, and somehow, through everything, you've thrived and created an incredible family. How did you do it? I really want to know and understand."

Ashley took a deep breath. "Well, it seems to me that in so many divorces, one parent moves out physically and the other parent checks out emotionally--leaving the children practically orphaned."

Paul nodded in agreement and listened intently as Ashley continued. "Each ex spends so much time licking his or her own wounds, they don't even notice the children's pain." Ashley looked very pensive. "I was determined not to do that. I put my children's welfare first, and it's paid off tremendously," Ashley said with gratitude.

"I'm fascinated you were able to understand how to do all that. And to act on it amid and despite all your emotional trials," Paul admitted.

"Thank heaven literally. I do have to credit lots of prayers. God really comes through when we let Him! But we must let Him. Some of my friends quickly found a new relationship. Now they have trouble with their children, trouble with their ex, and trouble with the new romance or marriage. It's a mess for everyone," she explained.

Paul got a serious look. "Many of those relationships probably started in a bar and ended up not as expected. Alcohol tends to cloud people's judgment."

Ashley and Paul laughed. "It happens a lot," Paul said. "At first, it seems so exciting. Prince Charming has finally arrived. All your dreams are coming true. Only to be shattered by reality. It happens to guys, too. Years ago, one guy described it well. He said, 'I went to bed with Sleeping Beauty and woke up with a moose.' He was serious. He could not figure out what had happened. I suggested alcohol was probably the most likely culprit. It often is. But instead of taking a new approach, people don't recognize or blame their own choices and do the same thing all over again."

Ashley smiled. "So, Einstein was right when he said that repeating the same thing and expecting a different result is insanity?" she asked astutely.

"Yep. Good call. Unfortunately, most people don't learn. We often end up unknowingly being our own worst enemy, as they say, and doing ourselves in. Ironic, huh?" Paul looked at Ashley intently. "You are incredible. After being abused and molested as a child and ending up in such a violent marriage, the odds were tremendously against you living any normal life. And yet you escaped that bad situation and are living a good and stable life. You also have such fantastic kids, as well. It is astounding."

"Well, thank you. And, yes, I would believe the odds were against me. All three of my older sisters were also molested as kids, too. They're all crazy." Ashley sighed in despair. "One refuses to have children. One gave all her children up. And one allowed her kids to be repeatedly molested by her husband. I had to testify against her in court for the sake of the children. It was awful!" Ashley rubbed her forehead. "We didn't speak for years, but occasionally we talk now. I was only a young teenager, or I would have taken all their children."

"You are amazing!"

"No. I just make my logic override my emotions, or ego, or revenge." Ashley laughed. "I try to learn from watching other people's mistakes. That and I have two secret weapons."

"'Secret weapons?' What are they?" Paul was very curious about Ashley's phrase and anxiously awaited her answer.

Ashley chuckled. "Well, the first one is that when I was growing up, I didn't like being in the house, so I spent most of my time outside, away from my sisters. We had grapevines that grew the whole width of the backyard. There was wooden framing that was about four feet wide, and it had metal fencing attached on top that held the vines. So, the bunches of grapes would hang down through the openings of the fencing. It was so tall that the adults had to stretch their arms to reach up to pick the grapes. One end of the frame had a swing attached. So, I would sit on the swing and hold onto the ropes in each hand, and I would swing up as high as I could to grab grapes to eat. It was wonderful. I felt like I was flying. I was the only one who ever used the swing.

"I liked being outside. It was a perfect escape. And I loved swinging. We had white grapes and purple grapes. However, I always wondered why they were called white grapes. They looked rather greenish to me. Sometimes, it was a bit scary letting go of one of the ropes to pluck the grapes, but it made me feel brave.

"It was a great escape from everything bad. I loved feeling the wind on my face and in my hair. I still do. I often take the kids to the park, and I swing as much as they do. It's great for your sanity." Ashley laughed. "I must admit, though, I really miss the grapevines."

"What a great story, Ashley. So, swinging is your first secret weapon. Very creative. What a terrific way to escape. And the grapevine addition is awesome. I like it, and I can see how it would bring you lots of peace and joy," Paul smiled. "And I love that you hold on to your inner child and still swing. We all need to do that. Having fun is extremely important. So, what's your second secret weapon?"

"I don't know if I should call it a secret weapon. It is a category all by itself. The most powerful thing I could ever do. I finally started truly trying to live the Christianity my grandmother taught me. I've learned that prayer really does work. Surprisingly well, if you don't give up. It's the best thing I've ever done and has brought me way more peace than swinging ever could." Ashley smiled and looked at Paul. "To sum up about the kids, I do what's best for my children, and it ends up best for me too."

The next morning, Paul walked down the hospital hall to the nurses' station. He had a bit of a bounce in his step, although he was tired from such a late night.

"Good morning, Dr. Brandon," Sally greeted him.

"Hi, Sally," he replied.

"I see you're working another Saturday too, huh?" Sally grinned.

Paul smiled and nodded. "It helps the weeks run better. Plus, as you well know, when people need help that doesn't come with a weekends-off calendar." They both laughed.

Paul entered Carl's office. Carl immediately stood up from his desk.

"I'm glad you got here."

"How's Penny?" Paul asked.

Carl looked distraught. "So far, no change. Judith's got her in the warm water swimming pool. I still have mixed feelings about that scheme you two cooked up, but I agree it can't hurt." Carl shook his head. "Penny has lost so much weight, it's awful. Poor little thing. I hope this works." Carl held out some papers toward Paul. "This is the next-to-last item on the list we made. I don't want to have to resort to this bottom one." Carl pointed to the last item. "Do you have something in mind that isn't down here, like that actress bit? I certainly hope you do."

Paul patted Carl's shoulder. "Just a thought. I want to study Penny's chart again."

"I thought you'd memorized it by now." Carl smiled.

"Which nurse has spent the most time with Penny?" Paul asked.

"Connie Schmidt. She has a terrific manner, and I requested she be with Penny whenever she's working," Carl said.

"Is she here now?" Paul inquired hopefully.

"I don't think so, but her schedule is at the front desk," Carl said.

"I want to talk to her. A good nurse has great insight. Good nurses are often underrated–those who genuinely care. Unfortunately, many nurses discover they don't really like people. That's after they have completed their college degree and training. Certainly not good for a medical occupation. But after all that schooling, they stay on the job without liking human beings and often cause others misery. Dealing with textbooks and instructors is different from patient care. I think they should start with supervised patient care to see if this is what they want to do for decades, before doing all the schooling," Paul said.

"You're right. Good nurses are underrated. But it's like everything else, we always notice the bad ones and take the good ones for granted. Also, I like your suggestion of starting with patient care. The legal department wouldn't, but I do," Carl chuckled.

"I want to check out something that's been on my mind," Paul admitted.

"Connie wouldn't mind if you called her at home. She's terrific. I also need you to talk to a teen who attempted suicide, Courtney Mathews." Carl put up his hand. "She's not pregnant and not on drugs. But she refuses to talk to anyone."

"What room's she in?" Paul asked.

"Three-twenty-one. She's been restrained. She kept throwing things at the staff and trying to pull out her I.V.," Carl explained.

Paul shook his head. "Poor kid. She must be mad that you saved her. Can you check with her mom and find out her favorite soda?"

"Sure," Carl agreed.

~

Courtney was in her hospital bed with her wrists

strapped to the bed rails. She was chewing her lip frantically. Paul entered her room carrying a six-pack of sodas and closed the door.

"Hello Courtney, I'm Dr. Brandon. Dr. Denton asked me to stop by. I brought you some root beer," Paul said gently. "I hear that's your favorite."

Courtney was outwardly hostile. Paul untied one of her hands.

Paul looked at Courtney. "You don't need this, do you? Anyone who can keep silent for as long as you have, has lots of self-control." Paul put ice in a cup and poured some soda in too. "Especially when telling everyone off would be so satisfying. Would you like a straw?"

Paul put the soda can on the side table and nonchalantly picked up Courtney's wash basin. He handed Courtney her soda, and she took the cup. Simultaneously, Courtney tried to throw the soda at Paul's face, and Paul put up the wash basin, stopping the liquid. Soda fell all over Courtney and her bed. Courtney was aggravated but impressed by Paul's anticipation and quick reaction. Paul handed her a towel.

"Here's a towel. Would you like another soda?" Paul asked.

Courtney remained silent and looked away.

Paul stepped closer to Courtney and quietly said, "I'll make you a deal. If you talk to me, I promise I won't tell a single nurse," Paul paused, "or anyone else, for that matter, that you spoke. They'll never know. Not your mom either. I will tell no one. Not without your permission. You are in charge."

Courtney turned her eyes toward Paul, but not her head.

"I won't hurt you; you've been hurt too much already. I want to help," Paul said genuinely.

Courtney was puzzled by Paul's sincerity. She looked around the room but avoided Paul.

"Courtney, if you could punch anyone, just let them have it, who would it be?" he asked.

She stared sternly at Paul. After a long silence, she responded.

"You!" Courtney snarled.

Paul untied her other hand. "Go ahead, let me have it," he said.

Courtney hesitated, then she hit Paul once, then twice, and then she frantically hit his stomach, chest, arms, and hands until she began to cry. She sobbed.

"It's okay, Courtney, I'm going to help you," Paul assured her.

"You can't help me. Nobody can!" she bawled.

The nurses got Penny back into bed. "I was hoping something would happen," Judith said sadly, looking at

Penny, as she fought back tears.

"It still may. It was worth a try," Carl encouraged.

"Things must be incredibly bad if you are consoling me. Do you know where Paul is? It's almost eight o'clock, and I've got to go," Judith said and then smiled. "Ralph and I planned to eat out at six thirty, so he said he would pick me up at eight. He knows us so well."

Carl laughed. "Good system. Paul's still with Courtney. The nurse reported that he has not been out of the room once. He must be making some progress."

"I hope so," Judith sighed. "Please call me if there's any change. With anybody." Judith kissed Penny's head.

"Of course," Carl promised.

"Thanks. Good night, Carl."

"Tell Ralph I said hello."

Judith smiled and left. Carl walked up to Penny and began stroking her head.

"Scooter, how can we reach you? How can we let you know it's safe to come out? We'll take care of you. Please. You know you are still my favorite patient." A tear dropped from Carl's eye.

Paul entered the room. "Any change?"

Carl straightened himself. "None. Nothing at all!" Carl said, exasperated. "How's Courtney?"

"Can we go to your office?" Paul asked.

Carl stroked Penny's hair and patted her shoulder. "Sure." Carl turned back to Penny. "I'll be right back,

Scooter. Very soon."

Paul and Carl left Penny's room. Carl paused in the hall. "Well, did she talk to you?" Carl asked.

"Wait till we get to your office," Paul whispered.

"What, does she...work for the F.B.I.?" Carl asked.

They entered Carl's office. Paul looked around the hall and closed the door.

"We talked, but you can tell no one. Not even her mother, especially not her mother!" Paul looked at Carl seriously. "You and I are the only ones who can know."

"You can trust me," Carl said.

"I assured her of that. This won't last long. But for now, we must keep quiet. Her life and her well-being depend on it," Paul stated emphatically.

"Why did she try to kill herself?" Carl asked.

"She felt there was no other way out. Apparently, her mother has a parade of boyfriends who often take a liking to Courtney. Her mother won't stop it, even though Courtney has begged her," Paul disclosed.

Carl was appalled. "Her own mother? Poor kid. That's appalling."

"Courtney had tried to get help at school, but the counselor told her she'd be old enough to leave in a few years. Can you imagine how hard it was to ask for help, only to be met with that response? The counselor may have well just said, 'Remain quiet and take the abuse!'" Paul shook his head. "It's infuriating, and she should be fired!"

"No wonder the poor child attempted suicide," Carl said.

"It gets worse. She went to a local church and was turned away because she wasn't a member. The last straw, she called a help hotline and was told it was for drug problems only." Paul was angry.

"You can't be serious?" Carl said in frustration.

Paul nodded his head. "She decided to put a stop to it herself. She figured she couldn't be bothered if she were dead. Voila – suicide."

"Very logical decision. Considering everything, it was a genius move. Not a good move but a genius one," Carl reluctantly conceded. "Poor thing had to be so desperate!"

"We need to keep her in the hospital until we work out things. She feels safe here. Courtney can never go home," Paul declared adamantly.

Carl patted Paul's shoulder. "I'm so thankful you got through to Courtney. I sure needed some more good news. So does Judith."

"You can't tell Judith until Courtney gives permission. I promised. Where is Judith anyway?" Paul asked.

"She and Ralph went to dinner," Carl said.

Paul was panic-stricken. "Dinner! Carl, I've got to go."

"It's okay. I'm going back with Penny."

Carl and Paul hurriedly headed in opposite directions down the hall. Paul took his phone from his pocket.

Paul yelled to Carl, "Call me if there's any change with Penny's condition."

"Yes, I will," Carl responded and continued to Penny's room.

Paul called Ashley and explained that he needed to talk to Penny's nurse. Ashley listened patiently.

"Paul, I understand. We'll eat after you meet with the nurse, or even on a different day. It's okay. Whatever works out is fine," Ashley said kindly.

Connie Schmidt answered the door. She was very cordial and motioned for Paul to enter her house.

"Please, come in," Connie welcomed Paul.

Paul entered. "Thank you so much for meeting with me on such short notice."

"Sit down," Connie said. They both sat, and it was a bit strained.

"Thank you again for seeing me."

"Anything to help Penny. That dear child breaks my heart," Connie shared.

"Has she had any visitors?" Paul asked. "There are a grandmother and an uncle listed who live near here. But they wouldn't talk to us."

"No. No one has come. It's a disgrace!" Connie was already heartbroken that no one had visited Penny. Discussing it was hard for her.

"That's what I thought. So, they couldn't be a link to Penny. Which means there is only one other way." Paul sighed.

Carl was taking off his shoes in their bedroom. It felt good to be at home. Glenda called from the bathroom.

"Honey, I know you've got special cases. You always do, but you're going to get sick if you keep working these hours. Doctors need rest too," Glenda said lovingly.

Carl thought, and then agreed, "You're right."

The telephone rang. "I'll get it," Glenda said. "And if it's the hospital, you are not available. Hello. Hi, Paul." Glenda listened, and her smile dropped. She became somber. "You want to bring somebody to the dinner party? Why, of course. That's fine. We'll see you tomorrow. Good night."

Looking sad, Glenda hung up the phone. Carl put his hands on Glenda's shoulders. "Look on the bright side, dear. Possibly one of the females will get sick. Then you'll be back to matched sets."

Glenda smacked Carl playfully. "Oh, you."

Carl kissed Glenda's head and started walking out of the bedroom. "Where are you going?" Glenda asked.

"To fix you some warm milk with butter for the headache and sleeplessness you're about to get. I know you," Carl replied.

Glenda smiled. "I sure do love you."

There was a nice park close to the restaurant where Paul and Ashley had dinner. They were taking a stroll.

"Dinner was very nice. Thank you again," Ashley said as they walked.

"Yes, it was," Paul agreed. "You know, this is the first time I've taken a walk in more years than I care to remember."

"You've made my list," Ashley announced.

"What list?" Paul asked curiously.

"My list of good men. When I start feeling like all men are rotten or jerks, I read my list of good ones." They both laughed.

"Well, I'm glad I made the list. I can't tell you how much you've given me." Paul stopped walking and looked at Ashley. He almost kissed her, but he refrained from his impulse. "You've given me hope and renewal, knowing what you've been through and seeing what a good mother and human being you are. It's wonderful and extremely encouraging." Paul smiled, and they walked again.

The next morning, the hospital was quite busy. Judith walked by the nurses' station closest to Penny's room.

"You're here on Sunday too?" Nurse Kiley asked.

"Is Dr. Brandon here yet?" Judith inquired.

"Yes. He's in Penny's room." Nurse Kiley shrugged her shoulders.

"Thanks," Judith answered and headed to the room. As Judith walked, Nurse Kiley asked, "Should I send Dr. Denton in there when he arrives?"

Judith was startled. "Is he coming?"

"He called and said he's stopping by."

"Oh, thank you," Judith replied. She rushed to the door, knocked, and opened it.

"Paul?" she asked.

"Yes," Paul answered.

Judith was nervous. "I wanted to wish you luck and let you know I'm here if you need me."

"Thanks," Paul responded.

"And Carl is coming by. I'll try to talk to him. Keep him busy. Or something," Judith said in somewhat of a panic.

"Whoa. Good luck to you, too, then," Paul said with concern.

"Maybe we should have let him know what you're trying?" Judith hesitantly suggested.

"No. He would never have approved. Besides, ignorance keeps him totally in the clear," Paul responded.

Judith looked around and gestured with her hands. "So, where is he?"

"In the bathroom," Paul said.

Just then, the bathroom door opened.

"Bye," Judith said and quickly left the room. She entered the hall, closed the door, leaned back, and deeply sighed.

Ben, Penny's brother, slowly came out of the bathroom. Paul squatted down to be closer to him and took Ben by the arms. "Are you okay, Buddy?" Paul asked as he had practiced.

Ben nodded his head and gave a big sigh. "Yeah," he said.

Paul put one knee on the floor to get lower to Ben's level and talked as calmly as he could muster. "Ben, we really need your help. I know what a strong, brave boy you are, and that's just what we need right now. We need you to help us reach Penny."

Ben looked at Paul with his big brown eyes. Paul hoped he was making the right choice. "You see, Ben, Penny's body is in the bed, but the part that's inside of her that makes Penny special is hiding." Paul smiled gingerly at Ben.

"You mean like hide-and-seek?" Ben asked innocently.

"Yes. Just like hide-and-seek. That is the perfect way to think about it. I want you to think of Penny being down in a deep well or hole." Paul wiped his forehead.

"Before, there was this great big rock on top that wouldn't let Penny come up. But it's gone now. We got rid of it. But she's still down there, and I think you can help her come out of there."

Ben rubbed his eye with his tiny fist. "What do I do?" Ben asked Paul.

"Just talk to her the way you always do. Tell her you need her and that you don't want her to leave. Tell her you need her a lot. And that you love her."

Ben nodded his head, but he looked scared. He was scared. Courageously, Ben managed to say, "Okay."

Paul rubbed Ben's head. "Don't be afraid, because anything you do or say will help. I'll be right with you the whole time. Are you ready?"

Ben nodded. Paul took a deep breath. "Then let's do this. Let's go get Penny," Paul encouraged Ben.

Chapter Seventeen

Desperation!

Carl knocked and peeked inside Courtney's hospital room. "May I come in?" he asked.

Courtney slightly nodded for him to enter while keeping her scowl. Carl came inside the room and gently closed the door. He walked closer to Courtney.

"I'm Dr. Denton. Thank you for letting Dr. Brandon share with me that you talked to him. Absolutely nobody but the three of us will know that. You are in control of any steps we take. Just like Dr. Brandon told you. We want to help you. You'll see. I promise."

Carl was thankful for the coaching Paul had given him on how to talk to Courtney. She was unsure of Carl. Courtney quickly felt good about Paul after the soda splattering. However, it would take time for Carl to earn her trust.

Carl understood Courtney's hesitancy. "I brought you a cheeseburger and fries," he said, handing her the bag. "I know you have a stash of root beer to drink." Carl smiled, trying his best to be comforting.

"Thanks," Courtney guardedly replied and took the bag.

"You're welcome. I don't think you have a cholesterol problem, and the food here isn't the greatest. There's something about hospital food and school cafeterias. Not the best," Carl responded.

Courtney trusted Paul. So, with the cheeseburger and fries, she decided to give Carl a chance. "That's for sure," Courtney said.

Carl chuckled. "Between you and me, I think it's the nutritionists. Restaurants and hotels don't have them, and they have great food."

Courtney laughed. Carl hoped it was the beginning of much more happiness to come. He desperately wanted to help.

"I've got to do a few other things, but I'll be back. Is there anything I can bring you?" he asked.

"I'd like some gum and potato chips. And some sort of listings for the TV. I want to spend the rest of my life right here. I never want to leave," Courtney admitted.

Carl smiled. "We'll get you somewhere that's even better. You'll see. Just give us a chance."

Judith had paced the hall outside Penny's room for some time. She mumbled to herself, wishing she understood more about prayer, or God, or something that would offer her comfort. She considered herself a Christian and tried to do the right things. However, she only prayed occasionally and rarely attended church.

Judith began talking to herself, a habit she had developed during stressful times in college. "This must work. Oh, please let this work. If this doesn't, we've lost her. We're out of ideas and running thin on hope. Patience is not my virtue. Carl, stay away. I don't want to hear your lecture."

At that moment, Judith saw Carl coming down the hall toward her. "Oh, no," she groaned and tried not to get sick.

"What's happening?" Carl asked.

Judith froze. She rapidly played out different scenarios that would happen depending on how she responded. Carl looked concerned.

"Are you okay?" he asked.

"Oh, yes. I'm fine," she replied as she bit her fingernail. Judith knew she could stall no longer. Carl was too savvy. "We're doing Paul's plan B," she said and tried to smile.

Carl thought for a moment. "Wait a minute. Plan A

was that phony mother. A for actress. What's Plan B?" Carl sincerely asked.

"In Paul's defense, I'm the one who wanted to use 'A' for actress," Judith confessed and tried desperately to know what to say. "You know how I like things to be orderly," she said and managed to buy a smidgen more time.

"So, what is Plan B?" Carl asked directly.

Judith knew she had to answer. "A for actress and B for Ben." Judith grimaced.

"He's got Ben in there? Is this guy certified or certifiable?" Carl was livid.

"Now, Carl, Penny's condition is so bad it's worth a try. What do we have to lose?" Judith asked.

"Ben, that's what! That kid has been through too much already. I'm stopping this right now," Carl said and stomped toward the door.

Judith quickly stopped Carl. "Please, Carl, give them some time. I think Paul's right. It's gone this far, let them at least try."

Carl angrily looked at Judith. "Ten more minutes and that's it." He looked at his watch and walked away.

Paul and Ben were still in Penny's room. There was so much emotion present it could practically be held in your hands.

Ben was sitting close to Penny on her bed. He had tried talking to her about everything he could think of to say. Ben became increasingly more upset, breathing heavily and swallowing between words.

"Penny, please. I want you to play with me. I miss you." Ben looked at Paul for reassurance. He became even more upset the longer Penny did not respond.

Paul whispered, "It's okay, buddy. You're doing great." Paul motioned for Ben to continue.

Ben breathed more heavily. "Penny . . .." Ben wiped his nose with the back of his hand. "I'll give you . . . my fire engine . . .." Ben kept swallowing, trying not to cry. "And my Legos, too - if you'll just . . . talk to me!" Ben screamed. He jumped up on his knees and straddled Penny. He started shaking her. "Penny, you gotta talk to me—you just gotta!" Ben was crying hysterically and screamed as he was still shaking Penny. "Penny, don't leave me! Please don't leave me! Please, Penny!" Ben sobbed.

Paul was an emotional wreck. He felt Ben was Penny's best chance of recovery, but he hated seeing the little guy in so much torment and emotional turmoil.

Suddenly, Penny began to stir slightly. Paul held his breath as he watched intently. This was the first movement he had ever seen in Penny since he met her. All the reports listed no movements whatsoever since the shooting.

"Ben?" Penny faintly questioned. Ben threw his arms

around Penny's neck. He hugged her and sobbed.

"I knew you wouldn't leave me. I just knew it!" Ben said between nose sniffles and sobs.

Paul stood by the bed with his eyes closed. Tears streamed down his cheeks. He thought of Ashley's comment regarding faith. At this moment, Paul knew God was very real. Paul fully recognized that neither medicine nor luck were this powerful.

Carl and Judith entered the room. Paul wiped the tears from his face with both hands.

Carl saw Penny and was shocked. Paul walked over to Carl and Judith. They were both stunned. Penny was attempting to hug Ben, but she could not even lift her arms. Ben just kept hugging and holding Penny. The three adults basked in the joy filling the room.

"What...." Carl uttered, then fell silent. Judith was sobbing. After some special moments and many tears, Carl began to move from his frozen position and spoke. "Thank God," he said.

Paul took a deep breath, looked at Carl, and replied, "I just did."

Chapter Eighteen

Lessons Lived, Lessons Learned...Maybe

Carl was on the phone in his office. "Glenda, great news. I have another single male coming to the dinner party. Now, you're back to matching sets. He's only six, but he's a giant." Carl smiled exuberantly.

Paul was talking to Ben in Penny's room, as Judith watched. Connie Schmidt checked Penny's I.V. and enjoyed seeing Penny awake, aware, and moving. She had cried many tears of joy when she learned Penny was conscious.

Paul lovingly touched Ben's cheek. "Well, trooper,

thank you again for all your help. You are fantastic. You take care of our little patient here, and I'll see you both later."

"Can Penny have ice cream too?" Ben asked.

Nurse Schmidt giggled at the joyous question and answered. "Not yet. She'll need to start with some broth first."

Judith pointed to Ben. "You can have all the ice cream you want, and so can Penny, just as soon as she's better."

Paul smiled at Judith. "I'm going to see Courtney. Do you need anything?"

"A celebration," Judith answered immediately.

"Me, too. See you at Carl's tonight," Paul agreed.

"By the way, I'm glad Courtney agreed you could consult with me, even if she doesn't want to meet me yet. With what her mother has done, it's important to have a female involved and helping too." Judith hesitated. "Ah, before you see Courtney, can you come to my office for a question that's been bugging me? Truly, it's been driving me nuts," Judith admitted.

"Sure," Paul said curiously.

Paul was sitting in Judith's office, and she said, "So, tell me about Hitler. I've been thinking about it ever since you made that comment, and you've got me so curious," Judith laughed. "Go figure. I liked learning about Solzhenitsyn. Maybe I just had some lousy history teachers."

Paul chuckled. "Could be. History is extremely important to know, so the bad stuff never gets repeated! On the front of the National Archives, there is a quote from Abraham Lincoln. 'What is past is prologue.' Meaning the past will be repeated unless we are aware and vigilant. We need to be cautious and learn from the past. And we need to be wise enough not to repeat the same mistakes, sins, and horrors. Onto your lesson," Paul smiled, then hesitated.

"Wait. I've got it." Paul was excited. "How about I tell you of five men connected to Hitler and WWII. I doubt you've ever heard of them. Since you're not crazy about history, I think you'll find this interesting," he suggested.

"Sounds good. Go for it," Judith nodded.

"I'll preface this by saying that the following is to the best of my knowledge after years of study. Now, for the first of those men: Did you know that a Roman Catholic priest and journalist, Bernhard Stempfl, played a significant part in helping with and editing the book that Adolf Hitler wrote that brought him much notoriety?"

Judith shook her head as she listened intently.

"In fairness to the priest, maybe he felt sorry for Hitler and was duped. After all, Mein Kampf means 'My Struggle.' And what was the thanks the priest got for helping Hitler? Stempfle was murdered as part of the killing in the 'Night of the Long Knives.' There were at least eighty-five people murdered that night, but it's possible there were more than seven hundred deaths on that night's killing spree. All of them were opponents and critics of Hitler and his Nazi crew."

"That's terrible!" Judith exclaimed.

"I've always thought that Bernard was killed so no one would know he helped with the book. Hitler would not look so commanding, having needed assistance. But I don't know who ordered Bernard's death. There were various people involved.

"Hitler, of course, was absolute evil. Calling the Jews parasites and every awful, demeaning term he could use. Which is incredibly ironic because Hitler pushed the fictional idea of the Aryan race propaganda. Hitler himself did not even meet that criteria, which was and is ironic.

"However, when you look at the whole historical picture, it appears Hitler was also a puppet and a stooge. That's the main point I wanted to tell you. There were people behind Hitler's rise to horror. They were funding him, teaching him, cheering him on, using him, and controlling much of the situation. That also included many photo shoots of Hitler to get the exact images they wanted for their creation.

"One of the main reasons that World War II happened is that after World War I, the Treaty of Versailles agreement that wrapped up that dreadful war said that

Germany had to pay reparations of approximately thirty-four billion dollars to the countries that were harmed and that had stopped Germany's aggression. That's billions with a B in 1919. This brings us to man number two. Wealthy German Alfred Hugenberg, businessman and media mogul, did not want to lose any of his money by having to pay for the destruction caused by WWI. There were also other rich German men.

"Hugenberg tried to form a committee to keep Germany from paying reparations. That failed. He then realized that to keep his money, he had to rally the working-class people. Hugenberg referred to Hitler as his 'tool.' That is important to know. With Hugenberg's media connections promoting Hitler, his popularity skyrocketed. Media can be tremendously powerful and sometimes a dangerous weapon. Hugenberg also got his wealthy friends to support and back Hitler. The way Hugenberg used the media to help create Hitler makes me extremely cautious and suspicious of today's current media and its mouthpieces and moguls. What are they truly trying to do or create? What is the underlying motivation?"

"Wow!" Judith said. "That's scary. I never knew or thought about any of that."

"You're right. It is scary! And there's more. Let's go to number three. Technically, Hitler was not German; he was from Austria. This fact alone prohibited Hitler from running for political office. Some devious political maneuvering was done. Dietrich Klagges, a bureaucrat, literally gave Hitler a non-elected title in government. That was the underhanded maneuver that led to Hitler receiving German citizenship, which he never should have been granted.

"Amazing how much evil can be created by so few people, huh?" Paul asked, and Judith, wide-eyed, nodded her head in agreement.

"This is absolutely petrifying! Especially knowing how horrible WWII was," Judith admitted.

"Absolutely. On to number four," Paul continued. "There was also a politician in this group whose task it was to 'create' Hitler. Franz von Papen, a nobleman who had been fired from the chancellorship. He missed being in the center of everything. After many meetings and covert deals, von Papen promoted the idea that Hitler be made chancellor and von Papen be appointed vice chancellor. Of course, von Papen did not expect Hitler to live long. We're getting to the final player in this awful creation that resulted in such tragedy throughout the world.

"Number five. The president of Germany objected to Hitler and his rise. However, he ultimately gave in and made Hitler the chancellor. President Paul von Hindenberg was eighty-five years old and not in good health. He had served two terms as president, and possibly they just beat him down to accomplish their desires. However, von Hindenberg never should have given Hitler that office. By doing so, von Hindenberg gave Hitler legitimacy because the people loved their president. That was probably planned to get the people to accept Hitler, which may not have happened without von Hindenberg's endorsement."

"Unbelievable! You make this stuff interesting. I wish I had known you in college or even high school. You also make it scary because it seems like the ordinary people were so easily duped." Judith was stunned. "Please, tell me more," she said.

"Well, it's also interesting that when the copyright ran out on *Mein Kampf*, there were those who raced to publish it with some commentary. My two favorite responses were: first, a historian from King's College London, Jeremy Adler, wrote, 'Absolute evil cannot be edited.' And second, Olivier Mannoni did a French version in 2021. He called the original 'an incoherent soup, one could become half-mad translating it.' For what *Mein Kampf* did and stood for, many scholars agree that Hitler's book should never be read, no matter what the reason."

"With the little I know, I agree with that totally! Those were great responses," Judith said.

"Yes, thankfully. What concerns me most is the group of men who made Hitler possible. Those men, all for selfish and evil reasons—money, power, whatever—ended up creating Hitler and World War II and the staggering death toll. I've seen numbers ranging from thirty-five million to sixty million killed. And it is usually not the people at the top calling the shots who pay the price in deaths of loved ones. It's the everyday, hard-working men and women.

"Evil is real and still here, and self-serving idiots are still around today. What are they willing to sell their souls for now?

"Remember when we agreed that individuals who don't learn from their mistakes are destined to repeat them?" Paul asked.

Judith responded, "Yes. That's always true and profound."

"It is also true of groups of people, countries, and nations. If we do not learn, we are destined to repeat deadly mistakes. That's why knowing history is important. Unfortunately, the cost of those mistakes is measured in lives taken. Over thirteen million were killed in WWI. These were sons and daughters, mothers and fathers, and children dead before their time. War is such a waste of life. Did we learn? No, there was another World War, again started by Germany. It is crucial to keep an eye on what all the countries in the world are planning.

"I strongly believe in defending yourself and defending our country. I know that freedom is the most precious, important, and valuable blessing we can ever have. It is well worth fighting for. That's why America is the best country—because it is the freest nation on earth. I just wish the fights would never start. The price that is paid is extremely high. God was quite clear—'Thou shalt not kill.' Some translations say 'Thou shalt not murder.' Either way, it is clear. Don't cause death. That's why I like Jesus so much. Try loving one another. We'll all be better off. And work for and accept forgiveness. Forgiveness is a gift that Jesus made possible.

"Don't get me wrong. We must always stand up for and protect our freedom and our country. That's majorly important, and we should never forget that. Sorry. I did not mean to get into all that. Wrongful deaths push my enraged button. There were so many prison inmates guilty of murder who had no conscience or remorse whatsoever. Frankly, it was nauseating. But I guess, when you join the devil and do his work and bidding, that's what happens. You lose your soul, sometimes before you ever even realize it."

"Paul, you are so right. Many of my patients start down the road to destruction by thinking they are having a great time. Drinking, partying, sleeping around, only to end up alone and a mess. They never see that coming. They usually blame the person they picked as a partner, but rarely do they blame themselves for making that bad choice of being with the wrong person. And they usually make that same bad choice repeatedly. When your mind is clouded by alcohol or drugs or even popularity, it's easy to create Prince Charming or Sleeping Beauty out of whoever happens to be there. But it's a creation, not reality. The happy ending never comes.

"Most start thinking all men or all women are rotten. Totally not accepting any personal responsibility for the rotten choices they made. They never take the time or put in the effort to make the necessary changes to find a good mate. There is no accountability for their bad selections. It's nuts.

"One of my biggest challenges is getting my patients to accept that good people truly exist. If you look for them under the right circumstances—no alcohol or drugs. And look in the right places—not in a bar full of drunks, you can and will find them. However, that entails a patient accepting personal responsibility for previously bad decisions. Not an easy task. The smart ones will finally recognize their mistakes and live a new strategy, making better choices. But many choose to wallow in self-pity, blame everybody but themselves, including God, and waste more of their life.

"As you pointed out, Satan is alive and well and a master at keeping people trapped!

"Boy, oh boy, when I think about it, we all need God! And to never forget Him! Now I love Solzhenitsyn too! Thank you for that," Judith declared with heartfelt sincerity. "I really wish I understood more about God and prayer. Sometimes I get unbelievably angry when kids are hurt and their innocence stolen! Or the sex trafficking of children! People don't realize it, but this is a very hard job.

"I believe there is a special, extremely torturous place in hell for all molesters. And for those who support them. Including just remaining quiet or looking the other way. Truthfully, I am counting on that future torture chamber in Hades. It is how I keep my sanity.

"Wow!" Judith laughed. "My turn to rant. I guess I have an enraged button too. Who knew?"

Paul chuckled. "Remember, it's good for the soul to get it out. Even yours." They both laughed, enjoying the release of deep, pent-up emotions.

Paul looked at Judith. "I need to get to Courtney, but you said you wished you knew more about God and prayer."

"I do," she replied.

"Before we go, I want to share some of what I learned from one of the ministers who visited the prison. There were pastors, priests, nuns, clergymen, clergywomen, and various religious leaders and their followers who came to preach to the inmates. They all seemed pretty much alike, except for this one minister, Reverend Clark. There was something about this man. You could feel something different about him. I didn't feel much from the rest of them, but I sure did with him. It was as if you could feel God with him or through him or something. He told me that feeling was the Holy Ghost testifying that he spoke the truth.

"He asked me if I ever prayed. I said I do. Then

he asked when and how I prayed. Do I pray when I'm driving to work and when I'm in bed ready to fall asleep? 'Yes, often,' I replied. Then he told me God was an 'afterthought' in my life. I only think of God after I've done the other things I want to accomplish. He explained to me that you do not get close to God praying that way. This man taught me more than I ever knew or understood before. He said we should put God first and pray respectfully. He pointed out that I would never treat my best friend or close family member in an 'afterthought' manner.

"He said, 'You would never treat those close to you that way. You make time for them, and you truly listen. You pay attention. You have a committed connection. That is something you cherish and nurture. It doesn't happen automatically; it takes genuine effort, sincere caring, and valuable time focused totally on that relationship.' He said God should be paramount in our lives and receive at least the focus, caring, and attention we offer our friends and family. We also need to pray first thing in the morning on our knees. Not after we've started our day and only work God in when it suits us. And we should pray on our knees at night before getting into bed. Not in bed, where we often fall asleep during our prayer. That one hit home big-time.

"He said we should put as much effort, if not more, into our relationship with God as we would a new romance. We should be that excited about creating and building a close interaction with Him. Of course, always praying 'in the name of Jesus Christ.' And closing with 'Amen.'

"I learned so much from him. He encouraged me to work on talking 'with' God instead of 'to' Him. Just like getting to know and be close to a person, it takes time and effort. And listening. Listening is crucial. Having a relationship with a person or God involves the same process. Desire, time, action, commitment, respect, caring, and effort.

"When I asked how many times a day he prays, he said roughly at least twenty. Two formal, on his knees, morning and night. But many times, throughout the day, he talks with God.

"I'm working on the two formal ones and an occasional prayer here and there. Nowhere near twenty. Not even four regularly. I have a long way to go. But I do feel a big difference.

"He pointed out something else that really made me think. He quoted John 3:16: 'For God so loved the world that He gave His only begotten Son… Do you completely understand what God and Jesus did for us?' he asked. 'God, our Father in heaven, loved us so much that He sent His only begotten Son to come here and be tortured and killed for us, for our sins! That through His sinless sacrifice, we can get forgiveness. That forgiveness is a gift! A gift for us. Justice was traded for mercy through Christ's sacrifice. Also, Jesus loved us enough that He was willing to come here and endure all He did for us. God and Jesus love us more than we can comprehend. The least we can do is work on having a relationship with God and accepting the gift of forgiveness that He made possible. And once you experience a real relationship with God and Jesus, you will never want to be without it,' he told me. I'm thankful I met him. And I do feel closer to God and Jesus than I ever did before."

Judith was taking in every word Paul shared. "I'm thankful you met him, too. I agree with everything you learned. Thank you for sharing," she said. "Boy oh boy, I'm a super 'afterthought' Christian. I've got some serious changes to make. I occasionally pray in the car, and that's it. Unless, of course, I have a problem. Then, I pray more until it's solved. And right back I go to my occasional car prayer, where most of the time, I get distracted and don't even finish what I'm saying. Not good."

Paul smiled. "But more typical than you think. I've come to realize that we are a pretty ungrateful species. And we tend to complicate life way more than it needs to be."

"You're right about that," Judith agreed. "Sounds like we should keep focused on the big picture. We need to lighten up and kneel down more, I would say. Thank you for sharing and clearing up my thinking." She smiled, nodding her head repeatedly. "Everything that minister said makes sense to me. I really want to work on not being an 'afterthought Christian'! Honestly, I'm barely even that. I even think understanding this perspective will help me in my counseling, too."

Chapter Nineteen

Look for a Bright Spot No Matter What

As Paul searched his office, he heard a noise. He stopped, listened, and then continued his search.

Where is that book? It's perfect for Courtney, Paul thought.

More noises came from the reception area. Paul went to investigate. He opened his door fully and saw Becky next to her desk. She had gotten caught in the rain and was dripping wet. Her hair was down and wet, and all her makeup was gone.

"Becky?" Paul questioned.

"Oh no, Dr. Brandon. What are you doing here so late?" Becky asked in a panic. Becky frantically tried to cover her face with her hair. "Don't look at me! I'm a mess. I'm just getting my jogging suit to go work out," she said, almost in hysterics. "I forgot it."

"Becky, calm down. What's wrong?" Paul asked.

"Don't look at me," she said. "Please, don't look at me."

Paul walked over and took Becky's arms in his hands, the same way he had done with Ben. He sat her down in her chair.

"Becky, stop. You look fine. You are pretty. As a matter of fact, this is the prettiest I've ever seen you," Paul observed.

Becky was completely shocked and unsure of how to react. "You're teasing me," she said.

"No. I am very serious. You're much prettier without all that makeup," Paul insisted.

Ben decided he did not want to go to the party at Dr. Denton's house; he wanted to stay with Penny and even spend the night there. So did Connie Schmidt. Neither of them ever wanted to leave Penny. They both wanted to stay right there until Penny could leave too. Carl made all the arrangements for now—including a small cot for Ben and a sleeping recliner for Connie—after everybody promised to get lots of rest and sleep.

It was a beautiful night. After their terrific and fun dinner party, Glenda and Carl were telling people goodbye.

"Glenda, you give the best parties. It was wonderful. The food was superb, and the games were great," Colleen said as she stepped off the porch.

"Thank you both so much for everything," Orlando, Colleen's new boyfriend, added. "Especially for introducing me to the new love of my life. It was love at first dance," Orlando said with a huge grin, pointing to Colleen.

Carl winked and smiled at Glenda. "One mission accomplished," he whispered.

Paul was off to the side and motioned for Judith to come closer. "I think I should prepare you," Paul said.

"Oh no, what now?" Judith asked.

"This is a good thing. Tomorrow, when we see Becky, I'm hoping there will be a change. That's why I was so late." Judith looked surprised, and Paul continued, "She'll be on shaky ground if she has the courage to try my advice. Becky will need all the help we can give her."

"How . . .." Judith started to ask.

"Sorry to interrupt, but this is my night with this lovely lady," Ralph, Judith's husband, said, joining them.

Judith smiled. "Isn't he terrific? Ralph took lessons from Carl, you know. See you tomorrow, Paul."

"I hope it's as good as today was," Paul replied.

Judith smiled, and she and Ralph left. Paul walked to Ashley, and they headed to the door where people were still mingling as they said their goodbyes.

Glenda greeted them. “We're so glad you could come. And don't worry about being late, Paul. You and Carl will both be late to your own funerals, as they say.”

Carl chuckled. “Being late for my funeral sounds good to me.” Everyone laughed.

“Sounds good to me, too,” Paul added. “But tomorrow's a working day.”

Glenda responded, “Aren't they all for you two?” Everybody nodded and looked at Carl and Paul with big smiles.

One of the guests elbowed Carl. “Glenda’s got your number big time,” he said as he left. They smiled and waved.

“Thank you for a lovely time,” Ashley said to Glenda.

“It's nice to see you, Ashley. Glad you could come.”

“Good night,” Paul and Ashley said simultaneously.

“Good night,” Glenda and Carl replied.

After the last guest had left, Carl closed the door, and Glenda picked up some dishes off the side table.

“Sweetheart, it's one in the morning; don't you think we should go to bed?” Carl proposed.

“It was a good party, wasn't it?” Glenda asked, ignoring Carl’s suggestion.

“It was a fabulous party. Now come to bed,” Carl said, pulling Glenda close to him and holding her tight.

"We can clean up tomorrow."

Glenda smiled. "And you were right," she admitted. "It is good for Ashley to get out, even though she won't marry again for many years, if ever."

"Yes, dear," Carl said.

"Thanks for not saying, 'I told you so.'" Glenda kissed Carl passionately.

The next morning, Becky was dressed more modestly than anyone at the hospital had ever seen her. She was also wearing very little makeup and a much more natural hairstyle. Becky looked genuinely pretty and nice.

Judith entered the reception area and was quite surprised, although Paul had tried to prepare her. "Becky?" Judith caught herself and paused. "You look wonderful."

"Do you really think so?" Becky asked in bewilderment.

"Definitely and wow!" Judith responded.

"It's scary. But Dr. Brandon challenged me to try this for a week. So far, so good," Becky smiled.

"Good for you. That took courage. And you are genuinely pretty. Much more than you realize, or than the rest of us could see before. I'm so glad you took Dr. Brandon's challenge," Judith encouraged.

Becky put her hands on her cheeks. "Thank you for

the kind words," she said sweetly with a smile. Becky was extremely nervous about her new look and truly appreciated Judith's encouragement.

Judith could tell how uneasy and frightened Becky was, not hiding behind the phony persona she had created. "Just speaking the truth, which is always the best policy," Judith grinned. "I predict that in a short time, you will be glad you took this challenge." She pointed to Paul's office. "Is he in?"

Just then, Paul stepped out of the elevator. "Good morning," he greeted them.

"Good morning. Do you have a minute?" Judith asked Paul.

"Of course," Paul responded and followed Judith toward her office. "Good morning, Becky," Paul said as he passed her desk.

Becky smiled, and Paul gave her a thumbs-up, a nod, and a smile of approval. Becky beamed as Paul and Judith entered her office. Judith motioned to the chairs, and they both sat down.

"I've been wanting to show you something. Please tell me if it's dumb. You and Mickey Mouse have inspired me to share something I've been playing with for months," Judith admitted. She opened a folder and showed Paul what she had written. He began to read.

To everyone:

Please take the time to write a letter that describes who is responsible for your bad choices, and who can help make your life much better.

Then it said, Lift for Sample.

When Paul lifted the piece of green paper, he saw a huge capital letter U!

Paul started laughing hysterically. “Talk about brilliant. This is it and says it all! Simple, straight to the point, and remarkable. If people grasp this concept, we’ll all be out of a job. Wouldn’t that be wonderful?” Paul declared and started laughing again. “I love it.”

“I’m so glad you like it. I’ve been wanting to share it, but didn’t have the courage until Mickey joined us,” Judith confessed with a snicker. “Counselors have insecurities, too, you know.”

“It’s great,” Paul encouraged. “You should have it framed and put it in the reception area with Mickey.”

Judith smiled. “Well, not right with Mickey, but we’ll find a spot.”

“Good plan.” Paul grinned. “I’m headed to an appointment. Wish me luck,” Paul said as he rushed out of the door.

Paul had talked with Clare Benson earlier and arranged to stop by her home. His grave concerns for her daughter’s safety regarding her stepfather and the current situation he had recently discovered gave him tremendous trepidation. He arrived as planned but had to speed a bit to be on time. She opened the door to welcome Paul.

"Please, come in, Dr. Brandon," Clare said, motioning to the living room.

Paul was apprehensive but entered. "Thank you for allowing me to come so quickly, Mrs. Benson."

"I must say, I was surprised when you called," she admitted. Clare directed Paul to the living room chairs. "Sit down. I had the maid make tea before she left. You said you wanted to speak privately, right?"

"Yes, thank you for clearing the house," Paul responded.

They sat down, and Clare served the tea. "I've never heard of doctors making house calls in my lifetime. I thought that was something from yesteryear. Do you take sugar?" she asked.

"Yes, one please." Paul took the cup and saucer. "Thank you," he said.

Clare sat down as Paul took a sip of tea. Then he placed the dishes on the table next to him.

Paul sighed. "This may be difficult to understand. Please bear with me." He rubbed his chin, as he often did to think. "Generally, the way counseling works is that the counselor guides a person in a good direction. You can't lead them, or push them, or even take them."

Clare held her cup and watched Paul. She was not at all sure what he was talking about and smiled nervously to hide her confusion.

Paul continued, "The counselor should be just a directing force. Almost like the navigator of an airplane, helping the pilot follow a good and correct course." Paul rubbed his neck. "Good counseling teaches a person to pilot his or her life, but it takes time. Much of what people discover in counseling, ironically, was right there all the time. They just hadn't seen or recognized it." Paul touched his forehead. "Do you understand what I'm trying to illustrate?"

"I believe you're saying that counseling sometimes helps us know things we really already know, but we didn't know we knew them," Clare Benson summarized.

"Precisely. Well said. In the interest of time, I'm doing something totally out of the ordinary procedure." Paul searched for the right words. "I'd like to talk to you about something I believe you know. But are refusing to admit—even to yourself, because sometimes it's very hard." Paul stood up and paced as he talked. "Teresa could stay at the boarding school, and we could spend months or years doing counseling. However, she will eventually be grown, and your relationship will suffer greatly. Possibly beyond repair."

Clare looked perplexed.

Paul resumed, "Besides, it's my understanding, you've signed up to take in a foster child while Teresa is gone. A girl, eleven to thirteen years old?"

"Yes. I was hesitant, but finally Harold convinced me. He feels it's our duty. He's so good."

Three hours later, Clare's living room was a disaster. Lamps, vases, clocks, and furniture were broken and thrown everywhere. Clare Benson was furious. She paced and ranted. Her friend, Michelle, sat on the couch and listened.

"I can't believe it! That wretched Dr. Brandon. I will get him fired yet. I've registered complaints everywhere." Clare hit her fist against the chair. "Can you imagine? Saying my Harold, my wonderful Harold, has a problem! That he's a danger to Teresa, and he needs help."

Michelle was uneasy. She started to shake.

Clare continued her rant. "I'll sue, defamation of character. That's what I'll do."

Suddenly, Michelle slammed the pillow she was holding against the couch. "Clare, stop it!" Michelle shrieked. "He's right, and you know it. Or you should know it." Clare was shocked. "Why do you think I won't let my Wendy spend the night with Teresa anymore? Or even come over here unless I'm visiting."

Nervously, Michelle started picking up broken glass, then she paused and looked directly at Clare. "You ought to be on your knees thanking God that that man cared enough to try and talk to you."

"But this can't be true, Michelle. You never said a thing," Clare said in anger.

"I was afraid . . .." Michelle looked around the room and did a swooping gesture. "Afraid of this. Oh, I thought about it. I even rehearsed it, but I never had the courage to face you. Count your lucky stars, at least somebody did."

Carl was in the reception area reading a report when a nurse entered.

"Dr. Denton, the chairman of the board is on the phone regarding Dr. Brandon. He said it's urgent," the nurse related.

"I'll take it in here," Carl said and entered his office. Carl picked up the receiver and pushed the flashing button. "Hello, Pat." Carl listened but was clearly irritated. "Calm down, Pat. I have the utmost confidence in Dr. Brandon and his judgment. I am positive there is an excellent explanation for all this. Goodbye."

The door was open, but Judith knocked.

"I've already heard all about it," Carl said. "Paul better have good reasons for these drastic actions."

Paul entered the savings and loan bank where Mrs. Renolds worked. He went directly to the receptionist.

"Is anyone in with Mrs. Renolds?" he asked.

“No. I'll see if she's busy.” The receptionist picked up the telephone.

Paul continued to walk back. “That's okay. She'll see me,” he said.

“But wait....” the receptionist objected.

“It's all right, I'll take full responsibility.” Paul opened the door. He entered, closed the door, sat down, and started talking to Mrs. Renolds.

Chapter Twenty

Under the Grapevines

So, on and on Paul went. He visited patient after patient, case after case—the strong ones, who he felt could and should be able to handle it. Paul addressed the problems involving children or teens, where time was so essential.

Paul stuck his head in Judith's office. "Becky said you wanted to see me."

"Yes. Please, come in," she said.

Paul closed the door and sat down. "I bet it's been a busy day here, huh?" he said with a grin.

"The phone has not stopped ringing, including the chairman of the board. Have you lost your mind? What is this, plan 'C' for crazy?" Judith asked.

Paul laughed. "Will you stop with the alphabet. And it's not C for crazy; it's C for crack-down. Something I should have done before now," Paul earnestly insisted.

"What?" Judith asked.

"I've made helping kids my main priority. It's a vicious cycle; our conventional route takes so long that the children or teens end up wrecked by the time the parents are straight."

Judith nodded in agreement.

Paul talked emphatically. "Then, years later, the kids are adults in therapy. And their kids are wrecks from having to deal with their broken parents. It may not work, but I'm taking a stab at breaking that cycle."

"You are going to get us all sued or shot," Judith warned.

"Nope," Paul assured Judith. "Everybody is off the hook. I put in my resignation early this morning. I'll be leaving in two weeks. Moving on. When you see Mickey Mouse, hopefully you'll remember me."

Judith gasped in shock. "Oh no, Paul. You didn't?"

"Yes, I did. But right now, I have one last stop to make. It's an extremely important one. So, I'll come by your house, and we can talk tonight."

"But—"

Paul interrupted Judith and kissed her on the cheek. "You're an A for angel," Paul said.

Judith chuckled. "I could never forget you!" she said. "You're incredible."

Paul entered the Rec Center and raced into Ashley's office. He was all smiles.

"I want to hire you," Paul declared.

Ashley was shocked and baffled. "What?"

Paul continued. "I have a real estate lady locating a large farm with a stable full of horses. I'm setting up a private practice there."

"Are you serious?" Ashley asked.

"Yes, and I need your help to make it work. I'm petitioning for custody of Penny and Ben. Oh, and Courtney. You don't know about her yet. I need to get her permission. Long story. And anyone else who needs to be there. I want a place where the kids can be safe and happy. And be kids! However, I need a female to be part of this to make it work; one who understands the garbage that sometimes transpires in life. But who also knows that you can transform the bad into a wonderful existence. I need an assistant. And your background and accomplishments make you perfect."

"Are you serious?" Ashley asked, and Paul nodded fervently. "That's an amazing plan!" Ashley paused and took a deep breath. She thought hard.

Then Paul said, "Of course, we'll need some other staff to participate as well. And guess what I am having added to the farm?"

Ashley looked at Paul. "I don't have a clue. What?"

Paul grinned, "An enormous grapevine arbor and swing just as you described it. I want you swinging under the grapevines just like you did when you were a kid. I think that's a great example for everyone. We all need to have fun and nourish our playful side. It does no one any good to become grumpy and stodgy. Being dull and boring is not enjoyable or healthy."

Ashley gasped as tears filled her eyes. Her hand went to her heart.

Paul smiled. "Purple and white grapes, too. And we'll add lots of swing sets, climbing bars, and sliding boards for all the kids. And the adults."

Ashley gave a huge grin. "Yes! For sure, you can count me in," she enthusiastically responded, and was so excited. "Who could resist this? You're creating paradise!"

It seemed impossible that things were working out so quickly, but Paul was determined and unstoppable. Paul's real estate agent, Mary Zander, worked tirelessly to find the right acreage. She deeply believed in what Paul wanted to accomplish. This had become a mission for her and not just a sale. Mary found Paul the perfect spot very quickly, where he had dreamed of settling.

There were acres of beautiful farmland with rays of

sunshine, as horses ran in enormous, fenced fields. A huge house literally sat on top of a knoll with two barns and other buildings in the background. At one of the smaller buildings, goats frolicked in the grass. At another small building, hens pecked the seeds on the ground and attempted flight, as little chickens ran around having fun.

Even though Paul resisted, Mary believed so strongly in Paul's idea that she paid for some of the playground equipment with her entire commission from the sale to donate to Paul's undertaking. Mary said she wanted to be a part of this glorious adventure. She was insistent and won that battle.

So many changes had happened, a year had passed in a flash. Two more buildings were added, similar to college dormitories.

Judith and Ralph were in their car on their way to Paul's. They were traveling on a small and curvy road. The car leaned to the right.

"It's good you're driving." Judith laughed. "Ralph, I am so glad you are going to get to see this. It's unbelievably wonderful," Judith described, as they drove to Paul's new world. "I truly believe that Paul has found his soul and his purpose completely right here, at last."

When Judith and Ralph arrived, children and young

teens were running and playing with Paul, Ashley, Carl, and Glenda. Carl and Glenda had become unofficially adopted grandparents, spoiling and loving all the youth. Some older teens and staff members were chopping vegetables and grilling dinner.

As hard as Ben tried, he could not run fast enough to catch up with Penny. Courtney finally ran and picked up Ben. She ran so fast with Ben, she caught Penny and picked her up too. Around and around they spun, laughing as hard as they could. Eight more children and teens were running everywhere, playing tag. They were all having incredible amounts of fun, feeling safe and loved.

The adults were also feeling loved. Ben and Penny brought more love to Paul than he ever imagined possible. Courtney, as well. He could not imagine life without their hugs and laughter. That love multiplied and spread like magic to all those fortunate enough to ever be a part of this incredible place.

Off to the right, the carefully transplanted, mature, beautiful grapevines were there with grapes literally hanging from them, waiting to be picked. There was a perfectly placed swing on each end of the arbor. It was exactly as Ashley had described and Paul had promised.

In the distance to the left was a playground with a myriad of slides, swings, and monkey bars. Pushing the merry-go-round with the children laughing was

Mary Zander, Paul's real estate lady. She wanted to be a part of this plan and had searched for and purchased much of the equipment. Of course, over Carl's objections, Glenda was working on finding Mary a righteous husband.

Judith beamed. "Do you understand what I mean, Ralph? This is like a fairytale come true. As we were driving up here, that old Elvis song kept playing in my head, 'If I Can Dream.' My grandma used to play it and dance with me when I was a kid. She loved Elvis, and she appreciated his voice. And I know she would have loved Paul's farm idea. Fresh air and lots of sunshine for everyone. Not only are they raising fruits and vegetables, but also growing and nurturing souls and hearts. Yes, my grandma would love this. Plus, she was always fun and adventurous."

"I don't think I know that Elvis song you mentioned," Ralph admitted. "Are you okay? Or are we looking for a farm?" Ralph paused. "I don't know if my allergies can take it."

Judith laughed. "No, we're not looking for a farm. We're just basking in the delight that dreams do come true! You just have to make them happen. You can search for the song on the computer when we get home. It's well worth hearing. And we can even dance."

So, Paul began a whole new life. Some of Ben's courage rubbed off on him that day at the hospital. Ironically, instead of getting in trouble, Paul became the most requested counselor in the entire area.

Back at home, Judith smiled. "This must be plan 'D' for delightful," she said, as she and Ralph danced to her grandmother's favorite song, which was now also Ralph's favorite.

Ralph held Judith close to him and then did a fun twirl. He softly whispered, "This is delightful. You are delightful. And it is plan 'D.' But the D is for Dream. Because Dreams do come true," Ralph said with a huge smile.

The Beginning of More Love and Hope for Everyone!

Epilogue

Joy Can Be Contagious—Share

Judith pointed her finger and grinned. "You guessed it. Paul and Ashley eventually got married! He adopted her children, and they had a baby girl whom they named Paula. Ashley insisted on that name because it was Paul plus A for Ashley, forever making them one.

"Ben started this wonderful adventure. A piece of his heart went into Paul the day they played cars and talked at the foster parents' home. Then, when Ben courageously awakened Penny from her nightmare, he unknowingly also awakened Paul's soul and took a piece of Paul's heart into his. At that point, there was no turning back for Paul.

"Then, one look at Penny when she became conscious, and with the sound of her voice, a separate chunk of Paul's heart was now with Penny. He was making dramatic changes quickly and wanted to increase hope for all he could. Paul could feel something happening. He prayed fervently for strength, guidance, and direction.

Paul and Ashley also adopted Penny, Ben, Courtney, and many of the other children. They adopted them so they would be a permanent family, and the kids would feel safer and more loved.

"Ashley became a special supervisor over the Rec Centers and implemented various terrific programs. She only had to go there occasionally, which was perfect. As Paula got older, Ashley kept all the children and teens on the farm involved in sports, science projects, math advancements, exploration adventures, and art endeavors. However, her two main goals were promoting family unity and ensuring everyone had a personal relationship with God. She felt that the farm was a piece of heaven on earth, and she named it Paradise.

"Above Paul and Ashley's fireplace, in beautiful painted scroll writing, it says, 'Our Father in Heaven & Jesus Christ love us... and you, too!' Even though heaven is not supposed to be capitalized, Ashley insisted it be since all the other places she knows that are real get capital letters. Ashley knows that heaven is real, and she feels like they are already living there. Their life is what they made it--heaven on earth.

"Paul and Ashley helped countless children and teens over the years. Ralph and I adopted three of them, even though our initial limit was two. Now, we are considering number four—the perfect number, no middle child.

"God can dream much greater than any of us can imagine. We only must be willing to go along for the journey of a lifetime and an eternity. Finding one's soul and discovering one's true purpose sometimes requires courage, challenges, and an honest self-assessment.

"It is amazing how, when you let love grow in your heart, your whole life and world get so much bigger and better. Turn everything over to God and Dare to Dream! You will be thankful you did."

Working Together Helps

Do not be surprised if a molester is one of the nicest people you have ever known. That is a clever tactic abusers use to get close to children and teens. It is also an effective disguise, the old "wolf in sheep's clothing" routine. People are often in shock and disbelief when they discover what has been transpiring.

Child molesters are experts at befriending children and teens. They also befriend adults as part of their cover. **It is time we beat them at their own game. Keep an eye out for things that are possibly happening! You may be saving a life.**

If you are prompted to help, the following are four good ways to start.

1. Over forty thousand children and teens need homes and families across America. Yes, over 40,000! This is through no fault of the children or teens. Many have lost their families to drugs, incarceration, diseases, death, or any number of other tragedies. Other children and teens have unfortunately been unwanted and abandoned by self-centered, self-absorbed individuals or those who will not step up to do what they should. Countless children need loving, righteous families. If that describes you, please investigate fostering or adopting in your area. Or contact AdoptUSkids.org. They will help

you find the right match. ***You can reap blessings far beyond your imagination.***

2. If you feel a child needs help, SPEAK UP! Alerting a good school counselor is often all that is necessary or alerting the authorities.

3. Adults who have suffered traumatic childhoods or even adult trauma and have not had the opportunity for *good* counseling can find that talking about what happened can be of enormous help. Do not carry the burden alone. Talking with a trustworthy friend tremendously lightens the anguish. If you are that friend, you only need to listen and **never** betray any confidences shared. **Listening is a talent.** Also, **good** counseling is always beneficial.

4. Encourage anyone, including yourself, who has had a terrible experience or experiences to start writing down those hidden feelings and events. Letting those emotions and inner pain fall onto the written page is much better than carrying them with you day by day, hour by hour, minute by minute.

   Writing helps. *Everyone should try it.* A spiral notebook and a pen can bring the freedom needed and the escape you deserve. You can always burn or destroy the notebook when the time is right. Or keep it to recount your courageous journey to genuine happiness.

Let's work together to STOP child & teen abuse!

Caring people can truly help.

Every time you see a **stop sign**, think

Stand **T**ogether - **O**ffer **P**rotection! **STOP abuse!**

Helping children and teens is the most rewarding thing you will ever do!

Helping/befriending adults is also important and often helps their children and teens.

May God direct your valuable efforts and bless you for your caring actions.

~ A New Beginning for Many ~

How about you? Or someone you care about?

A very special thank you
to all those who helped make this book
possible: Shane, Bryan, Ann, Karis,
Leigh, Suzanne, Sharon, and, of course,
our Lord and Savior, Jesus Christ,
and our Father in heaven.

About the Author

Author J.E. Daniels weaves passion for powerful writing with topical life issues and struggles of the characters. Creating captivating stories, the reader is immersed in the life-changing events and experiences of these characters. What draws them into their situations? What or who makes the difference in their ultimate direction? Which choices lead to the best outcome?

J.E. has devoted much time over the years to helping troubled males, abused women, children, and problem teens. For example, at great risk from armed pimps, J.E has walked the streets of Los Angeles, encouraging runaways and prostitutes to make better choices for themselves – never meeting a prostitute who was not sexually abused as a child or teen.

Their stories now inspire some of the events in these novels. J.E Daniels also writes screenplays, self-help materials, and more.

A sincere message throughout much of these writings interweave a most important and impactful journey – the understanding that Jesus Christ is real and the encouragement of a personal relationship. J.E.'s writings reach those who have walked or fallen away from their faith with an opportunity to change direction. They also enable followers to share Christian principles woven into these stories and characters by simply sharing a book and opening the door for many.

Having moved from the suburbs of Washington, DC, J.E currently resides in the Raleigh, North Carolina area.

Other books by J. E. Daniels

MacDoogles

Sand Trap

Sometimes the Boogeyman is Real

Why is Jesus? And Why Should I Care?

To learn more about J.E. Daniels and these books, visit www.JEDaniels.com